NED, BOB AND JERRY ON THE FIRING LINE

CLARENCE YOUNG

Ned, Bob and Jerry on the Firing Line

CHAPTER I

THE SPY ALARM

"There's a German on the ground! Get him!"

The sun glistened on scores of polished bayonets, as sturdy figures, clad in olive drab, which matched in hue the brown of the earth, sprang from their trenches and rushed forward.

"Put some pep into it! Lively now! Get the Germans!"

There were dull thuds, and there was a ripping, tearing sound as the steel slashed its way through the tough cloth. Along the swaying line rushed the young soldiers, stabbing to right and left as they went.

Now their weapons were directed downward with deadly force, and they sank them into the forms on the ground with such energy that the earth beneath was torn and gashed, and the muzzles of the guns, to which the stabbing bayonets were attached, made deep impressions on the yielding forms.

"There's a German on the ground! Get him!"

Again the cry rang out, and again the rushing, charging line surged forward, and then there followed once more the thuds which told of the cold steel going through and through and—

Then from the center of one of the charging lines there came a laugh as a lad, having driven his keen weapon home with too much force, being unable to free it, raised on his gun a large sack stuffed with hay, the fodder bristling out of one of the gashes he had made.

"That's the stuff, Chunky! Go to it!" yelled his laughing comrades. "If you can't get a German any other way, stick him on the end of your bayonet, bring him back to camp, and feed him to death!"

"Silence in the ranks!" cried the sergeant who was drilling the young soldiers of Camp Dixton in bayonet practice. For this is what it was, and not a charge on some Hun position; though from the fervor with which the boys went at it, and the fierce commands of their officers, a person hearing, and not seeing, might be inclined to believe that it was actual warfare.

And it was, as nearly as it could be approximated, for the sacks stuffed with hay or other yielding material, suspended on framework as is a football dummy or scattered over the ground, were called "Germans," by the drilling officers.

And, at the command: "There's a German on the ground! Get him!" it was the part of the prospective soldier to rush at the recumbent sack and stab it through and through with all his might, trying to put into the stroke all the force he would put into a similar one when he should attack the enemy.

"You got your man all right, Chunky!" observed a tall, bronzed lad, standing next to the stout youth who had used his bayonet with such force that he carried off one of the sacks as a trophy. "You must be feeling pretty strong today."

"Oh, let up, can't you, Jerry?" begged the badgered one. "The ground was soft under that sack, and I didn't think the steel would go through so far."

"Well, do that when you get on the firing line in France and it will be all right," commented another lad, on the opposite side of the one addressed as Chunky. "I wonder how much longer we're going to keep this up?"

"As you were!" came the sudden order, fairly barked out from an instructing sergeant, and the boys in the particular squad which included Ned, Bob and Jerry, of whom more later, resumed the positions they had been in before the order to charge bayonets had been given.

Chunky, or Bob Baker, to give his proper name, managed to get rid of the encumbering sack on his weapon, and marched back with the others. They lined up at attention and waited for the usual instruction and correction that followed each charge, or other army practice.

"That was pretty good, boys," said the sergeant, as he glanced down the line, "but I'm sure you can do better. A few of you were a bit slow.

"Now sometimes it's all right to be slow, if you have plenty of time, but in this business of bayoneting Germans you won't have much time to spare, as you'll find when you get on the other side, which I hope will be soon."

There was a murmur to this same effect from all in the line.

"When you're using your bayonet, use it first, or the other chap may get ahead of you and—well, you know what will happen then," went on the sergeant significantly. "And when you pull your weapons out, do it this way," and, taking a gun from the hands of Jerry Hopkins, the sergeant illustrated what he meant, using one of the filled sacks as an enemy.

"There wouldn't be much left of a German to send home after he got through with him," commented Ned Slade, as the sergeant handed Jerry back the gun. "He surely has some poetry of motion—Sergeant Black has."

"That's the way I tried to do it," said Bob, to his chums, Ned and Jerry. "Only—"

"Only you must have been thinking you were going to leave your gun and bayonet sticking in the ground to mark the place, so you could find it the next time," interrupted Jerry with a laugh. For, the command "At Ease," having been given, the prospective soldiers were allowed to rest and indulge in talk. The sergeant was called to one side, while a lieutenant gave him some orders about further practice and instruction.

"Aw, cut it out!" begged Chunky. "Guess you forget the time you slept through first call, and had to do kitchen police for two days."

"Indeed I don't forget it!" laughed Jerry. "It isn't a thing you can forget so easily. But let it go at that. Only it did look funny, Chunky, and you'd have said so yourself if you had seen it—it certainly did look funny to see you rushing along with the sack on the end of your gun."

"Didn't you feel the weight of it?" asked Ned Slade.

"Oh, Chunky's getting so strong, since he has his three square meals a day, regular, that he doesn't mind a little extra weight," commented another lad who stood in line near the three chums.

The drilling sergeant turned to his men again, and once more sent them through the bayonet charge. Then came other drills of various sorts, designed to make the young soldiers sturdy and strong, to fit them for the strenuous times that loomed ahead in France—times to try men's souls and bodies. But to these times the lads looked forward eagerly, anxious for the days to come when they could go "over there."

"Whew!" whispered Bob to Jerry and Ned, between whom he stood as they marched across the parade ground. "If this keeps up much longer I'm going to be a wreck!"

"Oh, some chow will set you up all right," commented Ned.

"Oh, say that again!" sighed the stout lad. "Them words fill me with mad desire!"

"Yes, and you'll fill the guardhouse if you don't stop talking so loud in the ranks," warned a lad behind Bob. "Cut it out. The lieutenant is looking this way," he added, speaking from the corner of his mouth so the motion of his lips would not be observed.

Rapidly the young soldiers marched across the grass-grown parade ground, in orderly array, in the last of the drills that morning. The company to which Ned, Bob and Jerry belonged were drawn up near their barracks, and Captain Theodore Martin, after a glance over the two trim lines, turned the dismissing of the group over to the first lieutenant.

4

The breechblocks of the guns were opened, clicked shut again, and then came the welcome words:

"Comp sissed!"

That is what the lieutenant snapped out. But what he really meant, and what the members of it understood, was:

"Company dismissed!"

Ned, Bob and Jerry, with sighs of relief, which were echoed by their comrades, turned to stack their rifles and then prepared for "chow," or, in this case, the dinner mess.

As the three chums were heading in the direction of the mess hall where, every day, two hundred or more hungry lads and men were fed, they saw some members of their company turn and run in a different direction.

"Hello! what's up?" asked Jerry Hopkins, coming to a halt.

"Matter where?" inquired Ned.

"Over that way," and Jerry pointed. "Either somebody is hurt, or there's a riot."

"Let's go!" cried Ned.

"Wait until after grub," advised Bob, with an anxious look toward the mess hall.

"It won't take but a minute," suggested Jerry. "Look, everybody's going. We might as well be in it. If everybody is late to mess there'll be enough left for us to eat. Come on!"

Accepting this argument, that such a general rush toward the scene of excitement would result in a general postponement of the meal, Bob, after a moment of hesitation, joined his two chums. They rushed toward one of the sleeping barracks, and saw that a large crowd was congregating around it.

"What's the matter?"

"Anybody hurt?"

"Is the place on fire?"

These were some of the questions that flew from one to the other.

"It's a spy!" some one said. "They've caught a German spy in camp, and they're going to lynch him!"

"Oh, boy!" yelled Ned. "We must see this!"

"I don't believe it!" announced Jerry. "There've been too many German spy scares. They all turned out to be fakes. And, anyhow, there won't be any lynching."

"Maybe not," agreed Bob. "But there sure is some excitement."

And there was. Even Jerry had to admit that.

As the three Motor Boys—to give them the name by which they had been known for some time—neared the barracks, the rumors and statements as to the capture of a spy became more frequent and certain. There was an excited, seething crowd about the place.

A lieutenant, whom Ned, Bob and Jerry knew well, as he came from their town of Cresville, passed just then. The three chums saluted, and, when this had been returned, Jerry asked:

"Can you tell us, Sir, what it's all about?"

"Have they really caught a spy?" added Bob eagerly.

"Well, whether he is a spy or not I can't say," was the answer. "But I have been told that a man, who was acting in a suspicious manner about the camp, has been arrested. Some of the officers are investigating now. I hardly think he will prove to be a real spy, though."

"He won't last long, if he is," commented Ned.

"They have him in the barracks there," went on the lieutenant. "They will bring him out soon, I suppose, and put him in the guardhouse. Better go back, boys," he added. "There's too much of a crowd here now. I must help disperse it."

He turned away, but the advice he had given Ned, Bob and Jerry was not very welcome.

"This is our sleeping barracks, anyhow," said Ned. "We have a right to stick around, and go in, too."

"If they let us," added Bob.

"Come on, let's try," suggested Jerry. "Here's a place," and he led the way through a thinning portion of the crowd toward one of the doors of the big wooden shack, in which he and his chums slept while at Camp Dixton.

Suddenly there came a series of excited shouts from within the building. Then several soldiers were seen to rush out as though something had chased them.

"What in the world is up now?" asked Jerry of his chums.

6

They pressed forward toward the door from which the excited soldiers had emerged, and one of them, seeing that the three chums were about to enter, cried:

"Don't go in there!"

"Why not?" asked Bob.

"Did the spy try to shoot any one?" Ned wanted to know.

"Don't go in!" yelled another lad. "There's a snake in there as big as a barrel, and he's skipping around as lively as a kitten! Keep out if you don't want to meet sudden death. Oh, boy! I saw him open his mouth, and one look was enough. No more for me!"

CHAPTER II

A MAN AND A SNAKE

Ned, Bob and Jerry paused a moment on the threshold of the barrack building they had been about to enter. From within came a sound of commotion, as if several persons were quickly rushing to and fro, and there were excited shouts.

"Come off, Jack, what are you doing? Trying to string us?" asked Ned of the lad who had spoken of the snake.

"Nothing of the sort!" protested the other. "As true as I'm telling you, there's a snake loose in there as big as a barrel, and as long as a fence rail around one of these cotton plantations!"

"Is he joking, Ted?" asked Jerry of another of the lads who had rushed out in such haste.

"Not a bit of it! I saw the snake myself. It isn't quite as big as a barrel, but it certainly is long."

"Come on, fellows!" called Jerry to his two chums. "We've got to see this!"

"What!" cried Jack Wade, "you aren't going in there, are you?"

"Why not?" asked Jerry. "We've had some experience with snakes. Besides, we want to see the spy. Is there a spy inside here, too?"

"There is!" cried another lad. "They caught the spy dead to rights, planting a bomb under the officers' mess building. Wanted to blow 'em all up when they were eating, I guess. Oh, he's a German spy, all right, and they have him tied up!"

"But what connection has he with the snakes?" Bob questioned.

"Not any that I know of," replied Jack.

"Yes, he has, too!" asserted one of his chums. "The spy had the snake. He was going to let him loose in camp, hoping he'd bite and poison a lot of us, I s'pose, so we can't go to France to fight the Huns."

"Big snakes are seldom poisonous," cried Jerry. "This may be a python or a boa escaped from some circus, though I haven't heard of any animal shows being around here lately."

"Me, either," added Bob. "Say, are you sure you saw a snake?" he asked the lads who had rushed out in such a hurry.

"As sure as we see you now, and you're not much smaller around the waist than this same snake," added Jack with a laugh.

8

"Cut out the comedy stuff!" murmured Bob.

"Well, if there's a real snake in there I want to see it!" exclaimed Jerry. "Come on!" and he pushed open the door which had swung shut after the exit of the excited lads.

Within the barracks the three Motor Boys saw a scene of excitement. One end of the big building, which was filled with cots and bunks, was comparatively empty, but at the other there was a group of officers and men. Some of them appeared to surround the captive, though the three chums could not just then get a glimpse of him.

"There it is!" suddenly cried Ned, pointing.

"What—the spy?" asked Bob.

"No, the snake! See it?"

He pointed. There was no doubt of it. A long, glistening, brown body was seen to glide under a row of cots.

"It's a snake all right," assented Jerry, "but not half as big as I thought. It's just like one I've seen—"

He was interrupted by a voice which rang out above the murmurs from the group at the other end of the barracks, and the commanding voice of Colonel Shield demanded:

"What is going on here? What is all the excitement about?"

It appeared that he had just entered at the doorway around which were grouped the excited officers and men.

"We have caught a spy," some one said.

"He must have let the big snake loose!" another added.

"Well, why don't some of you shoot the reptile?" asked the colonel. "A fine lot of soldiers you are, I must say! Afraid of a snake! Where will you be when you go up against the Germans? Some one get a rifle and shoot the snake!"

At this command a protesting cry came from the midst of a group of soldiers who were guarding the man arrested as a spy.

"Don't shoot my snake! Don't shoot my pet snake!" came the entreaty. "He is worth a fortune! Don't harm him!"

There was a commotion—a scramble. Several men stumbled and fell, and from their midst a figure dashed—a figure at the sight of which a gasp of astonishment came from the three Motor Boys.

9

And since Ned, Bob and Jerry have been called Motor Boys several times I will take just a moment here to tell who these lads were and something about them; also why they were at Camp Dixton. Of course, the readers who already know this may skip what immediately follows and proceed with the story.

As related in the initial volume of the first part of this series, a book which is named "The Motor Boys," Ned Slade, Bob Baker and Jerry Hopkins were chums of long standing. They lived in Cresville, not far from Boston, and the three lads were well-to-do. Jerry's mother was a wealthy widow, while Bob's father was a banker, and Ned's a department store owner.

The Motor Boys were so called because they spent so much time in or about vehicles that depended on gasoline motors for their activity. They began with motorcycles and ended with airships—though one should not say ended, for their activities were far from over.

In the books succeeding the initial volume are related the various adventures of the Motor Boys, who journeyed to Mexico, across the plains, and traveled much on the Atlantic and Pacific, both in craft on the surface and in submarines. Their trips above the clouds in aeroplanes and airships were much enjoyed.

"The Motor Boys on Road and River," was the last volume of the first series, the final volume to carry that title.

The second series began with "Ned, Bob and Jerry at Boxwood Hall," and the only change in the stories was in the title, for the main characters were still the "Motor Boys."

The parents of the lads felt that they ought to do some studying, and, accordingly, Ned, Bob and Jerry were sent to Boxwood Hall. What took place there formed not only a well-remembered part in their lives, but furnished some excitement as well. When vacation came they went to a Western ranch and had fun, as well as helped in an important piece of work.

And then came the Great War.

Our heroes could do nothing less than enlist, and in the volume called "Ned, Bob and Jerry in the Army," which immediately precedes this one you are reading, is told something of their life at Camp Dixton, one of the training camps in the South.

There the chums had learned to become soldiers, and, with others of their kind, were eagerly awaiting a chance to go over seas and fight it out with the Huns.

And now we meet them again in the midst of excitement over a spy scare—not the first of the kind to happen in the camp, where, as the readers of the volume before this will doubtless recall, the activities of "Pug" Kennedy and "Crooked Nose," formed the basis for some real danger.

"That snake sure is real!" cried Bob, as he saw the serpent writhing about. "And whoever has him for a pet must be nervy."

"Look! Look!" exclaimed Jerry. "The spy is going right for the snake!"

"And look who the spy is!" added Ned.

There were shouts from the officers and men. Several of the latter had gotten their rifles and were edging about, trying to find an opening through which they might fire at the serpent.

The man who had broken away from his captors rushed toward the end of the building where Ned, Bob and Jerry had last seen the reptile, which was now out of sight under some bunks.

"Don't shoot him! Don't shoot my pet! He is worth thousands of dollars!" cried the reputed spy.

And then, to the surprise and fear of all save the Motor Boys, who had an insight into the truth, the man fairly threw himself forward on the serpent, as a football player falls on the ball.

"Ah, I have you! I have you, my beauty!" cried the man. "You shall not get away from me again, and they sha'n't shoot you, either!"

CHAPTER III

A PUZZLED PROFESSOR

For a moment there was comparative silence in the big barrack building. It lasted while the little man was crossing the room and hurrying toward the big snake where it could be discerned under a line of bunks. The words uttered by the owner of the serpent were heard by the three chums, as well as by every one else in the building.

And then, as the small man continued on his way, and finally launched himself at the snake with outstretched hands and arms, some one uttered a warning yell.

"Look out!" came the cry. "It's only his bluff! He's trying to escape. Catch the spy!"

"That's right!" shouted several, who seemed to agree with what had been said.

But if the little man—the "spy" as he had been called—had it in mind to escape, he was taking a queer way to go about it. For even as a rush toward him on the part of those from whose midst he had escaped began, the little man arose and held clasped in his arms the snake—or as much of it as he could raise from the ground. On his face was a look of anxiety relieved, and he fairly beamed on those who confronted him. His former, and would-be, captors had again come to a halt. Almost any ordinary body of men and boys would have done the same under like circumstances, for there is an inherent fear of snakes in almost every one.

"Get him! Don't let the spy escape!" came the cry.

"Yes! Let's see you get him—with that snake for a protector," murmured one.

"I don't mind getting shot at by a German," said a voice, "but I'll be jiggered if I want to be bitten by a snake."

"Shoot the snake!" came the cry.

"No, please don't, I beg of you!" pleaded the little man in a mild voice that, somehow, carried to the far end of the room. "Please don't shoot the most valuable snake I ever owned. Really she is quite harmless; aren't you, Ticula?" and he looked up at the swaying head of the snake that was weaving above him, as though to ask the serpent to speak.

"Ticula!" burst out Ned. "Is that her name, Professor Snodgrass?"

The little man started, and peered through his glasses in the direction of the voice.

"Ha! It seems there is some one here who knows me," he said. "I cannot see him, but I seem to recognize the voice."

"I should think you would," chuckled Ned. "We've traveled with you often enough, Professor. But this is a new one—a pet snake as long as a lasso."

"And named Ticula!" added Jerry, with a laugh.

"Oh, that is only a name I made up for her out of her own proper, Latin one," explained the professor. "Her real name is Python Reticulatus; but I call her Ticula for short. And, unless I am greatly mistaken, it was Jerry Hopkins who spoke to me that time. Am I right?" and he peered about rather uncertainly, for the corner where the three chums were standing was in deep shadow.

"You are right, Professor," said Jerry. "And we are as much surprised to see you here as to 'meet up' with your snake, as the folks in the South say. What brought you here?"

Before Professor Snodgrass could answer—and it has been, perhaps, guessed before this that he was the "spy" referred to—a sudden movement on the part of the snake made it necessary for him to devote some attention to his "pet" as he called her.

Ticula seemed uneasy at being stared at by so many eyes, and she began to writhe and twist as though anxious to escape. There was a sudden scramble on the part of the soldiers and officers in the barrack building, but the three chums, having faith in their old friend, the little scientist, did not retreat.

"There now, Ticula," murmured Professor Snodgrass, in what he doubtless meant to be soothing terms, "no one shall harm you. You're excited on account of getting out of your box, I suppose. But I'll soon have you back there."

He reached up, and began to stroke the snake back of the weaving head, and gradually the forked tongue, that had been playing in and out with the quickness of lightning, was quieted. Ticula seemed to regain her composure. She settled down, wrapping a fold or two about the little man, who did not seem at all alarmed at the movements of the snake, though one officer murmured:

"Great Scott! he's taking an awful chance. That's a constrictor, and it can crush an ox!"

But Professor Snodgrass gazed mildly through his glasses at those surrounding him and inquired:

"Are you all three there—Ned, Bob and Jerry?"

"All present and accounted for, Professor," answered Jerry, with a laugh. "And now that Ticula seems quiet, perhaps you'll explain what it all means."

"Yes, I think an explanation is very much in order," said the colonel, who had urged some of his men to shoot the snake.

"First let me get my pet back in her sleeping box," said the little scientist. "She will be quieter then. If one of you gentlemen will have the kindness to bring me the box you took away from me, I'll put Ticula to sleep."

"Bring in the box," commanded a lieutenant. "We caught this man, Sir," said the lieutenant, addressing the colonel, "hanging around the officers' mess hall with a box. We thought it contained an infernal machine, and that he might be a German spy. We brought him here to talk to him, and then we discovered the snake crawling around. The box is outside."

"Have it examined and brought in," said the colonel. "It is just possible," he added with a smile, "that the prisoner is what he claims to be—a naturalist. Is there any one here who knows him?" he asked.

"Yes, Sir," answered Ned, Bob and Jerry in a chorus.

"Come forward and explain," ordered the colonel.

The three chums advanced and saluted. Professor Snodgrass seemed to be having a little trouble quieting the snake, which had again raised her head and was hissing at the crowd in front of her. Some explanations were necessary, it would seem, and Ned, Bob and Jerry seemed the best qualified to offer them.

"We know Professor Snodgrass very well, Sir," said Jerry. "He has often traveled with us, and we have helped him in his collection work. He is connected with some of the largest museums, and goes about getting rare specimens for them. He is no more a German spy than we are."

"Glad to know it," commented the colonel. "Do you know anything about this mysterious box he had?"

"No; but it is probably what he says it is—a cage for this snake, Sir," explained Jerry. "He has any number of specimen boxes and cages when he travels."

By this time some of the men had brought in the box in question. It was painted green, and was about three feet long—in itself rather a good load for one man to carry, not so much on account of its weight as because of its shape, but with the big snake inside, one man could not have lifted it.

"That's a snake box," said Jerry, after he had examined it, "but it is a new one—I never saw it before."

"No, I had it made especially for Ticula," explained the professor, who had again succeeded in quieting the serpent. "Now, my little pet," he went on, "I'll put you to bed."

The box was brought forward and set down on the floor in front of the professor. The man who brought it dropped it quickly and made a hasty retreat at the nearer sight of the reptile.

Then the scientist gently lowered the serpent's head toward the box, which was lined with cloth. The snake seemed to recognize her quarters, for, without hesitation, she coiled herself down in the case, the perforated lid of which was then closed.

"There, now she is all right," said the professor. "I shall not let her loose again until to-morrow, and then—"

"What?" yelled a lieutenant. "Are you going to turn her loose around here again?"

"Why not?" asked the professor. "The observations I hoped to make to-day as to her feeding habits in the open have been spoiled because you arrested me as a spy. I could not conclude my experiments, and I must continue them to-morrow. But do not be alarmed. Ticula, though rather large, is perfectly harmless to man. Indeed, she has not yet gotten her full growth. She is only fifteen feet long, and her kind often grows to twenty-six feet and weighs nearly two hundred pounds. Ticula is a mere baby."

"Some baby!" murmured a voice, and even the colonel laughed.

"And now I suppose I am at liberty to go with my property?" asked the professor, looking around inquiringly.

"Well, since it seems that you are not a German spy, I fail to see that we have any reason for holding you," returned the commandant. "As for the snake, I think the men—and I may say myself—would feel obliged if you did not turn it loose again."

"Well, I suppose I can select some other place for my experiments," murmured the professor, in rather disappointed tones. "But this spot was ideal. There are so many rats and mice about a camp of this sort that a snake or two would be very beneficial."

"I have no doubt," said the colonel dryly. "And yet, somehow, I think I prefer the rodents. But I should be glad to have you explain further just what your experiments are in reference to your reptile. I am interested. I shall be

15

pleased to have you lunch with me," he went on, for, now that he had a chance to observe, he saw that Professor Snodgrass was a cultured gentleman, as well as, he presumed, a devoted scientist. The colonel was something of a student himself.

"I should like to lunch with you," said the professor, "but my three friends— Ned, Bob and Jerry—are here and—"

"We'll see you later," whispered Jerry. "We're enlisted men and can't mess in the officers' quarters. You must dine with the colonel and we'll see you later."

"All right," assented the professor, and accepted the colonel's invitation. "Help me carry Ticula out to my auto and I'll see you after dinner," he went on to the boys.

"Have you an auto here?" asked Bob.

"Yes. I left it just beyond the confines of the camp. I have an old friend of yours with me, too," he went on. "He helped me carry my snake here."

"An old friend?" murmured Bob.

"Yes, Pete Bumps who used to be your father's hired man. I've engaged him as a helper since you boys joined the army. He runs my auto for me and helps me catch specimens. He isn't afraid of snakes."

And old Pete Bumps it was who greeted Ned, Bob and Jerry as they accompanied the professor to his car.

Pete had left the Baker service some time ago, and had secured a place as janitor of a college in which the professor taught, he briefly explained to the boys. There the professor had engaged him just prior to starting out on his present expedition.

"Come on. We've got to hurry back to mess," said Jerry to his chums. "But we want to have a talk with you, Professor, after you finish dining with the colonel. We want to hear what you are doing here again. I should think once being taken for a German spy was enough," and he laughed at the recollection of a former occasion, when the professor, coming to visit his friends at Camp Dixton, had been halted on his way through the lines after some insects.

"I never thought of that," admitted the scientist. "I certainly remember coming down here in the spring, but I forgot about the spy business."

This was not surprising, since the professor seldom remembered for very long anything not directly connected with his favorite study.

16

And so, with the snake in the box safely confined to the care of Pete Bumps in the automobile, Professor Snodgrass went back to dine with the colonel, while the three chums hastened to their delayed mess.

"You never know when he is going to turn up," remarked Ned.

"That's right," agreed Jerry. "I wonder what he's after now?"

They did not have long to wait before learning. Soon after mess they saw the professor coming down their company street and, as they had a brief respite from drills on account of the strenuous work of the morning, the boys took him to a quiet spot and began to ask him questions.

"But first of all, tell us if there is anything the matter?" begged Jerry. "You look worried. Are you?"

"Yes," admitted the little scientist, "I don't mind admitting that I am worried—and puzzled, too."

"What about?" asked Bob. "Ticula hasn't got loose, has she?"

"No, I went over to see, after dining with your colonel, whom I found to be a most delightful man, though his ignorance of reptiles and insects is painful. But, as I say, I assured myself of the safety of Ticula. Pete has her in the auto."

"Then what's worrying you?" demanded Ned.

"Well, I have a problem to solve and I don't know how to do it," was the answer.

"Has it anything to do with the war?" Jerry queried.

"Yes, it has," was the unexpected answer. "And now that you boys are in the army and expect to go across to France soon, perhaps you can help me. I'll tell you the puzzle I am trying to solve."

CHAPTER IV

A TWO-GIRL PROBLEM

Jerry Hopkins stretched himself lazily and comfortably out on the grass under the shade tree where he and Bob and Ned had taken Professor Snodgrass for a little talk. They were far removed from the center of the camp, so the noise of the men drilling or at their various occupations came but faintly.

"Do you mean that your problem has to be solved on the other side of the water, Professor?" asked Jerry.

"Part of it has. And I am anxious to get across as soon as possible to begin."

"What?" cried Ned. "You don't mean to say you, too, are going to France, Professor?"

"I hope to," was the answer. "I have arranged to go, and I have my passport and some letters of introduction."

"But what are you going for?" asked Bob. "Don't you know you will be in the midst of terrible fighting? You can't solve any problems there. It will be a bedlam of noise."

"And the noise is just what I want," said Mr. Snodgrass. "That is one of my problems—to find out the effect of noise on the organisms of certain insects and reptiles. Men suffer from shell shock, and why should not insects suffer from the terrific noise of bursting guns? Most insects are noise-producers themselves," he went on, in something of his class-room manner, which the boys so well remembered at Boxwood Hall. "The grasshopper, the katydid and the cricket, to give them their common names, each have a song of their own. These insects are found in France, as well as here, though in somewhat different form.

"Now I have a theory that a long-continued series of terrific noises may produce structural changes in insects, so as to change the character of their 'songs' as I prefer to call their sounds. This can best be studied on the battlefields of France, though I suppose I could get the same effect here, if there was a continuous thunderstorm with vivid lightning.

"But, as that condition is impossible to bring about, I shall best find it in France, and thither I am going, soon I hope. This snake experiment is only a brief one, undertaken at the behest of a friend of mine who is writing a book on the feeding habits of pythons."

"Is that what brought you back to our camp?" asked Jerry.

"Yes. This particular part of the South at this season of the year has the very climate suited to pythons and other large snakes of the tropics."

"I'm sure it's hot enough," murmured Bob, mopping his perspiring face. "I'm glad we got out of drill this afternoon. But go on, Professor. I didn't mean to interrupt you."

"Well, there isn't much to tell about the snake," said the scientist. "I purchased Ticula, as I call her, some time ago from a museum. She is a fine specimen of the regal python. Originally she came from Borneo, where she was captured when very young. As I stated, she has not yet attained her growth, and I have succeeded in making quite a pet of her."

"Deliver me from such pets!" murmured Ned.

"Ticula is not a venomous snake," went on the professor. "None of the constrictor type of serpents is, though their power to crush their prey in their folds is enormous. They depend on that power, while the poisonous snakes kill their prey by the use of their venom. But Ticula and I are quite friendly.

"My friend, who is writing a book on snakes, asked me to find out something of how pythons capture their food, and, knowing there would be plenty of large rats in the vicinity of a camp, on account of the great food supply there, I came here with my pet snake.

"I suppose I should have secured permission from some officer to let loose the serpent near one of the buildings, but I forgot all about it, thinking of the problem I have to puzzle over. I also forgot for the time being, that you boys were here at Camp Dixton, or I should certainly have communicated with you and got you to help me.

"But I went at it alone. Pete and I carried the box, with the snake in it, of course, close to one of the buildings. I did not know until later that it was the officers' mess hall. Then Pete left me alone."

"How did you manage to get through the sentry lines unchallenged?" asked Jerry.

"I don't know," frankly answered the professor. "I suppose it was because no one saw us; or they may have supposed we were bringing some supplies to one of the officers. Then, there was a sham battle going on not far away at the time, and that may have taken the attention of the sentries. Anyhow, I got through the lines, and, opening the box, let Ticula out to roam about and catch a rat if she could.

19

"I was crawling around after her, watching her as she went under the building when suddenly a soldier pounced on me and yelled that I was a German spy. I was never more surprised in all my life."

Jerry and Bob chuckled.

"I should think you might be!" laughed Ned. "Then what happened?"

"Well, they handled me rather roughly, and took me into custody, as I suppose it is called. They seemed to think Ticula's box was an infernal machine. They were very much excited, and I was trying to explain to them who I was, when Ticula suddenly crawled up through a hole in the floor in the building where I was being questioned."

"And then there was more excitement, I suppose," said Jerry.

"There was—considerable," admitted the professor. "Then you boys came in, and—well, it's all over now. But I surely feared for a moment they might shoot my snake."

"Yes, it was rather a close call," observed Bob. "But did you have a good dinner with the colonel?"

"Listen to him, would you!" protested Ned. "All he can think of is eating!"

"Cut it out!" growled Bob, as Ned poked him in the ribs. "I just wanted to know what sort of feed they give the officers."

"Oh," said Jerry significantly. "Merely an academic interest, I suppose."

"Sure!" assented Bob. "That's all."

"Well, the dinner was very good, though I cannot say that I remember what I ate," confessed the professor. "I was thinking too much of something else."

"Do you mean you were puzzled as to how to study the effect of the noises of the French battlefields on grasshoppers and crickets?" asked Jerry.

"No," and the professor shook his head. "This is an altogether different problem. It is, as I might call it, the problem of two girls."

"Two girls!" cried the three Motor Boys in a chorus. "Two girls?"

They looked at the little professor, whose eyes, mildly blinking behind his strong glasses, regarded the lads curiously.

"Two girls," repeated the little scientist. "The problem I have to solve concerns two girls."

CHAPTER V

MORE GIRLS

Ned, Bob and Jerry looked at one another. Then they turned their glances on the professor.

"Whew!" softly whistled Jerry. "Can it be possible that our dear friend is in love—and with two girls at once? This is getting serious!"

It would have been had Jerry's diagnosis been correct. But it was wrong, as was proved a moment later, when the professor, with a sigh, resumed his narrative.

"Yes," he said, "I am much concerned over two girls—young ladies I suppose would be the more proper designation. I have never seen either of them."

Jerry breathed more freely, and so did his chums. Clearly if the professor had not seen the two girls he could not be in love with them. And the professor in love was something unthinkable. He never would have remembered, from one day to the next, the name of the favored lady.

"And, boys," went on Professor Snodgrass, "I think you will agree with me that it is quite a problem to try to find in Europe, at this particular time, two girls I have never seen, that I may deliver to them a small fortune, and claim one myself."

"Say, this is getting worse and more of it!" cried Ned. "What does it all mean, Professor? Are you in earnest about these girls and the effect of war noises on insects?"

"I am in earnest about both problems—never more so," was the answer, and it needed but a glance at the face of the scientist to disclose this fact. "But perhaps I had better explain."

"Perhaps you had," said Jerry with a smile.

"And never mind about the insects—tell us about the girls," urged Bob.

"Yes, relieve his mind," agreed Ned. "He hasn't heard from his dear Helena in some hours, I guess."

"Oh, cut it out!" protested the stout lad.

"The two girls to whom I refer," went on Professor Snodgrass, "are the nieces of my late friend, Professor Emil Petersen."

"The man who wrote the book on trigonometry that we used to study at Boxwood Hall?" asked Ned.

21

"The same," murmured Professor Snodgrass. "Professor Petersen was an eminent mathematician, and the world did not fully estimate his worth. His mathematical work was only a branch of his many-sided activities. Professor Petersen died about three months ago, and he left me a most peculiar legacy."

"Peculiar in what way?" asked Ned.

"It is like this," said the little scientist, as he pulled up a blade of grass, and examined it under a powerful hand glass to see if any strange insects might be crawling on it. "Professor Petersen, unlike most of us professional men, was very wealthy. He was a Swede, and his wealth came to him from his father. He never used much of it, and the money accumulated.

"After his death I was surprised to learn that he had made me one of his heirs, but under certain conditions. It appears that in his younger days Professor Petersen was estranged from his brother and sister, on account of some family matters. They received an equal share with him from their father's estate, but they made unwise investments, and soon lost the major portion of their inheritances. The professor kept his. Perhaps that was one reason for the estrangement.

"At any rate, some coldness existed, and it was not until just before his death that the professor wished to be reconciled. Then it was too late, as his brother and sister were both dead. But each had left a daughter, and the young ladies were studying abroad—somewhere in France or Germany, I believe, when the war broke out.

"I was greatly surprised, when the will was made public, to learn that I was to have half the professor's not inconsiderable wealth, on a certain condition."

"And what condition?" remarked Jerry, as the professor hesitated.

"That condition is as follows. I am to seek out these two nieces of my dead friend and give them each a fourth of his estate. The other half I am to have for myself if I fulfill the trust. That is, I get it if I can succeed in finding the two girls, and I need not tell you that I shall be very glad of the large sum of money—not for myself, oh, no!" said Professor Snodgrass quickly, "but that I may devote it to the furtherance of the interests of science. If I can solve the problem, and find the two girls, I shall have a large sum at my disposal, and I can then fulfill a life-long desire to undertake the study of the insects of the Amazon River. That is what I have always desired to do since I took up my studies, but I always lacked the means. Now, if I succeed in finding these two girls, I shall have wealth enough to travel in South America."

"And where are the girls?" asked Jerry.

22

"Somewhere in Germany or France," was the answer. "The latter country, I think. I have, among my papers, their last address. But since the war there is no telling where I may find them. I have written a number of letters, but have had no answers. Now I must go to seek them, and, at the same time, make a study of the effect of battle noises on crickets and grasshoppers. Is it any wonder that I seem puzzled? Was there ever such a hard problem for a peace-loving scientist to solve?"

"It isn't going to be easy," admitted Ned. "Then you really expect to go across?"

"Yes. And since I understand you are going, we may go together; or at least meet there, for I suppose I shall not be allowed on a transport, being a civilian."

"Hardly," assented Jerry. "But if, as you say, you have passports and credentials and letters of introduction, it may be arranged. You had better see our colonel. He seems to have taken quite a notion to you."

"Thank you; I will," promised the scientist. "And now I think I had better go back and see about Ticula and Pete Bumps. Pete may be worried about me."

"Just a moment," suggested Ned. "If we are to help you in the search for these two girls, we ought to know something more about them."

"That is right," assented the professor; "and I hope you will help me. The problem of finding the two young ladies would be easy were it not for the war. But they have been missing since the conflict started, and I can get no trace of them. I hope they are still living, for, if they are dead, all the wealth Professor Petersen left goes to a humane society for the care of distressed cats and dogs and to provide a shelter for them. Not that I object to cats and dogs," he hastily added, "but I think some other form of scientific activity might be chosen. However, Professor Petersen was very peculiar, and, after all, it was his money. Will you boys help me?"

"Indeed we will!" cried Jerry. "But how are we to go about it? What part of France were the girls last in?"

"And what are their names?" Bob demanded.

"And what do they look like?" asked Ned.

"That last question I can answer first," said the professor. "I happen to have recent pictures of them. They sent them to their uncle following the deaths of their parents, and after the reconciliation, and Professor Petersen left them to me, with certain other material, documents and such, to aid me in the search. Here are the girls—their names are Gladys Petersen and Dorothy Gibbs."

23

He reached in his pocket and took out a folded paper. As he opened it he gave a start and hastily closed it again.

"That isn't it," he murmured. "Those are some dried specimens of ameba that I wish to study under a microscope."

"What are ameba?" asked Jerry. "Fish?"

"Not exactly," answered the professor with a smile, "though I secured these from a little pond on the other side of the camp. Ameba are microorganisms of the simplest structure—a protoplasm which is constantly changing in shape. Very interesting—very interesting indeed, but not the pictures of the girls. Ah, here they are," he added, as he replaced the first paper and took out a second. From the folds of that he produced two unmounted photographs at which the boys gazed with interest.

They saw the likenesses of two pretty girls in traveling costume, and the pictures had, obviously, been snapped by an amateur at some country place, for there was a barn and fields in the background.

"The girls took these pictures themselves, I understand," explained the professor. "They sent them to their uncle."

"Which is which?" asked Jerry. "I mean which is Gladys and which is Dorothy?"

"The names are on the reverse side of the photographs, I believe," said the professor, and so it proved.

"They are both pretty," observed Jerry.

"I rather fancy Gladys," murmured Ned.

"Dorothy seems real jolly," stated Bob.

"Here! None of that, young man, or I'll write to Helena Schaeffer, and tell her how you're carrying on!" warned Jerry, shaking a finger at his stout chum.

"Aw, you—" began Bob.

But at that moment there came an interruption. A small, very much excited lad came fairly bounding over the grass toward the figures of the three chums and Professor Snodgrass.

"Oh, here you are!" cried the newcomer. "Found you at last—thought I never would—asked everybody—nearly got stabbed by a sentry—had to jump out of the way of a bullet—whoop—but here I am—Gosh! Say, it's good to see you again—I told 'em I could find you—awful hot, ain't it? Lots of things

24

going on—never saw so many soldiers in all my life—here they are, girls! I found 'em!"

Ned, Bob and Jerry gazed in amazement at the small lad. Ned murmured his name—Andy Rush—and then Jerry, looking over the head of the excited little chap, descried three girls approaching.

"Girls! Girls!" murmured the tall lad. "More girls! What does it mean?"

CHAPTER VI

NODDY NIXON

Events were transpiring so rapidly for Ned, Bob and Jerry in the last few hours, that it was no wonder they were somewhat startled. Coming from strenuous bayonet practice to hear of a spy alarm, to have that augmented by excitement over the big snake, to learn that the "spy" was none other than Professor Snodgrass, and then to hear of his strange mission, would have been almost too much for any group of lads less sophisticated than this trio.

And hardly had they digested the news about the two missing girls, in a search for whom they mentally agreed they would join, than along came excitable Andy Rush and—more girls.

"There's Mollie Horton!" cried Ned, recognizing a girl who lived near him in Cresville, and with whom he was very friendly.

"Yes, and I see Alice Vines," added Jerry.

"And Helen Gale is with her," commented Bob. "I'm glad she came! Helen's a great girl for sport and—"

"You'd better be careful how you talk," warned Jerry, as the girls continued to approach. "Helen and Helena are names very much alike, but if you get them mixed up—well, Helen isn't one to stand any nonsense."

"Aw, say—" began Bob, and then the nearer approach of the three girls, to whom Andy Rush was beckoning, put a stop to any further talk concerning them.

It might be added, to explain Jerry's reference, that Helena Schaeffer was a girl in whom Bob Baker felt more than ordinary interest. At first, because of the pro-German leanings of her father, she had been a bit cold toward Bob when he joined the army with his chums, to fight the Kaiser. But, as readers of the volume preceding this know, Helena changed her attitude, much to Bob's relief.

"Well, of all the sights that are good for sore eyes!" cried Ned, as he hurried forward to greet the girls, an example followed by his chums. "What fine wind blew you here?"

"We didn't come in an airship!" burst out Andy Rush. "I wanted to, but they wouldn't—'fraid they'd fall—swoop up—swoop down—get here quicker—fall maybe—maybe not—lots of fun, anyhow. Gosh, it's great—I say, fellows, are you going—"

Jerry gently but firmly took hold of Andy by the ear, and, pointing to Professor Snodgrass, who was wandering about a distant field in search of possible insects, said:

"Andy, you go and aid in the interests of science, and, incidentally, cool off. We'll see you later."

And Andy, whose rapid flow of words had been suddenly stopped, looked once at the tall, bronzed lad, and then followed the instructions to the letter. So, whether he wanted it or not, Professor Snodgrass had the assistance of the small youth.

"Well! Well!" exclaimed Jerry, as he shook hands lingeringly with Alice. "How did you get here?"

"Going to enlist?" asked Ned.

"Maybe they're going to join the girls' motor corps," suggested Bob, who had attached himself to Helen.

"No, we just came on a visit," explained Mollie.

"To see us?" asked Ned.

"Of course!" was the mischievous answer. "We got lonesome back in Cresville, with all the nice boys gone, and so we got Andy to bring us down here."

"And if we believe that, I suppose you'll tell us another," laughed Jerry. "Seriously now, how did you happen to come, and how long are you going to stay? Fellows, we'll have to get furloughs and take the girls around. Not that there's much to see down here, but we'll do our best," he added.

"Cease! Cease!" commanded Ned, holding up his hand like a traffic officer in front of Jerry. "Let's hear how they happened to come."

"Oh, that is soon told," remarked Alice. "Mollie's aunt lives not far from here."

"And she invited Mollie down on a visit," added Helen. "And Mollie was good enough to ask us, so we all came together. We reached there yesterday, and, knowing you boys were at camp here, we decided to come out to see you, which we have done."

"And for which we are duly grateful," added Jerry. "But what about Andy Rush? I never was more surprised in my life when I heard his usual flow of language. How did he happen to be with you?"

"That was just an accident, a coincidence, or whatever you want to call it," said Mollie, with a laugh. "When Andy heard we were coming down this way

27

he asked if he couldn't come with us. He says he is going to enlist. He isn't going to wait to be drafted. He said he'd sort of look after us on our way down."

"But it's been the other way about!" laughed Alice. "We've had to watch him all the while. He was always hopping about, talking to strangers, and every time the train stopped at a station longer than a minute he'd get off, and we'd be in a fix for fear he'd be left. But he's here, thank goodness!"

"Going to enlist!" cried Ned. "Why, he's too small."

"That's what they told him back in Cresville when he tried it," remarked Alice. "But we must give Andy credit for being a determined little chap. He's sixteen, and he says lots of boys of sixteen have gone in, and he's going. He said if the recruiting officer at home wouldn't take him one here at camp might. So he came with us, and I believe he's going to ask you boys to use your influence to get him into the army."

"A heap of influence we have!" laughed Ned. "Privates—with Jerry just made corporal."

"Well, Andy was very nice to us on the way down," said Helen, "so please do all you can for him."

"We will!" promised Jerry. "And now tell us about yourselves, and how all the folks are at home. Oh, but it's great to see you again!"

Then followed a talk until it was time for the three chums to report for drill duty.

"What are you girls going to do this evening?" asked Bob.

The girls looked at one another.

"Oh, just sit around, I suppose," remarked Mollie.

"No, you're not!" cried Jerry. "There's a dance in town—a really nice place— and we've been wishing for some girls to come along to help us out. It's under the auspices of the local Y. W. C. A. And if we can get off—"

"Oh, we'll get off all right!" broke in Ned eagerly.

"If worst comes to worst, we'll have the professor ask the colonel on our behalf. The prof seems to pull a pretty good stroke with the C. O. So a dance it is to be!" declared Bob.

And a dance it was. The boys received permission to remain away from camp until midnight, passes being issued to them, and they at once proceeded to "doll up," as Bob expressed it.

A joyous week followed, for the girls were to remain in the vicinity of Camp Dixton, at Mollie's aunt's house for some time, and they asked nothing better than to have the company of the three chums as often as it might be possible.

Of course, Ned, Bob and Jerry did not have very much time to themselves during the day, and some of their nights were occupied. But fate was kind to them, and they had several dances with the girls, and also went to "shows" at the local Y. M. C. A., as well as entertaining the girls by escorting them about the cantonment.

Meanwhile, Professor Snodgrass received permission to loose his pet snake, Ticula, in certain restricted areas, so that he might observe her feeding habits in the open.

"But I cannot stay here very long," he told the boys. "I must soon begin to prepare for my trip to Europe. I simply must make an attempt to find those two girls."

"And we'll help you!" declared Jerry. "Just wait a few days more. I think our orders to go across are coming."

And come the orders did. The day before the three home-town girls were to return to Cresville orders came for the larger part of the soldiers at Camp Dixton to leave for France.

"Hurray!" cried Ned, Bob and Jerry, as they saw the orders posted. "Now we'll get a whack at the Germans!"

"And I'm going, too!" declared Andy Rush. "I'll go if I have to leave as a stowaway! I've simply got to fight—get me a gun—let me go in an aeroplane—I want action—got to do something—can't keep still—Hurray for Uncle Sam!"

"Say, you'll burst a blood vessel if you aren't careful!" cautioned Ned. "Better go slow, Andy."

But Andy Rush was not the lad for that, and he hurried about the camp, more excited than ever, seeking for a chance to go abroad.

Ned, Bob and Jerry, with thousands of their chums, were to go to Hoboken, New Jersey, there to go aboard a transport and be escorted to France. By a stroke of good luck, and by pulling some official, or scientific wires, Professor Snodgrass received permission to go on the same vessel. He hurriedly sent his pet snake to a museum to be cared for until his return, mailed his specimens of ameba to a scientific friend to be made into microscopical slides, and then, having fitted himself out with as many specimen boxes and other paraphernalia as he was permitted to take, announced that he was ready for his dual mission—the seeking out of the two girls that he might apprise them of their good fortune and to undertake the study of the effect of war noises on crickets and katydids.

The final drills, bayonet practices, hikes and other camp activities were held, and then the order came to break camp. Professor Snodgrass went on ahead, promising to meet the three chums in Hoboken, and Mollie, Alice and Helen departed for Cresville, their good-byes to the boys being rather tearful, it must be admitted.

As for Andy Rush, he disappeared on the day when the young soldiers were to take the train for the North, and no one seemed to know what had become of him.

"Guess he found he couldn't get in the army, and he went back home," remarked Ned.

Finally the three chums were on their way for the fighting front with thousands of fellow soldiers, some being volunteers and others of the selective service.

Many and varied were the thoughts of our heroes as the train bore them northward. What would be their fate in France? Would they ever see home again, or would they be left across the water with the others who died that civilization might live? And mingled with these thoughts were others as to the mission of Professor Snodgrass.

"It surely is some commission—trying to find two girls with just their photographs and nothing much else to go by," commented Ned.

"But we have done harder things," added Jerry.

The journey North was rather tiresome, but the boys and their companions enlivened it as much as possible by singing, telling stories, and general activities.

Once, when the train was delayed at a junction the three Cresville friends got out, as did hundreds of others, to "stretch their legs." There was another train-load of young soldiers on a siding, having come from another camp, and lads from this were also walking up and down.

As Ned, Bob and Jerry stood together, looking at a group of recruits who had been trained in Texas, they heard a voice saying:

"This drafting business makes me sick! I don't like it at all!"

"Maybe you'd rather have been passed over," suggested some one.

"Naw, you get me wrong!" was the answer. "I want to fight all right, but I want to do it my own way. I'd have enlisted in the air service if they'd given me time enough. I was thinking of it when the draft law went into effect, and then I couldn't. I know a lot about airships. I used to run one, and I invented one, too."

"Did it fly?" some one wanted to know.

"It would have if it hadn't been for some mean fellows in my town who didn't want me to beat them," was the announcement. "You wait until I get on the other side! I'll show 'em what flying is, if they give me the chance, and Jerry Hopkins and his pals sha'n't stop me, either!"

"Did you hear that?" asked Ned in a low voice.

"I should say so!" exclaimed Bob. "We ought to know who that is."

"Noddy Nixon, without a doubt!" remarked Jerry. "And up to his old tricks! I hope he isn't going on the same transport with us!"

CHAPTER VII

OFF FOR FRANCE

Noddy Nixon needs no introduction to my old readers. This rich and impudent lad had, more than once, done his best to injure the Motor Boys, and, with the plotting of Jack Pender and Bill Berry, a Cresville n'er-do-well, had too often succeeded.

"Well, I don't see anything of Bill or Jack," observed Jerry, as he looked toward Noddy Nixon, and noted, that the bully was surrounded by a group of strange recruits.

"Yes, if he's by himself he won't be so hard to handle," agreed Ned. "But I wonder where he came from? He ought to be in jail!"

"I suppose he came from some training camp—same as we did," observed Bob. "And he looks as though he had been well fed, too. He's as fat as butter."

"That's Chunky all over—thinking of the eating end," laughed Ned.

"Yes, Noddy is fat all right—too fat!" declared Jerry. "He hasn't been drilled as hard as we have, or else he got a desk position somewhere and held on to it."

"Did you hear the bluff he was throwing about trying to enlist in the air service?" asked Ned.

"Yes," agreed his tall chum. "Talk about his being an expert flier! Say, do you remember his Tin Fly?"

"I should say so!" laughed Bob. "The flying machine that wouldn't go up. That was a hot one! But keep quiet—he's looking over this way."

Noddy, indeed, seemed to have his attention attracted to the three friends. At first he looked uncomprehendingly, and then, as the features of the lads toward whom he had acted so meanly became plainer, he stared and finally exclaimed:

"What are you fellows doing here?"

"The same as you, I imagine," was Jerry's cool answer. "We are going to fight in France."

Jerry said afterward he wanted to add that he and his chums had "volunteered" to do this fighting, but he did not think it would be quite fair to the drafted men with Noddy who, to do them justice, were in the same class as the best of patriots. The selective service law solved many problems, but Noddy's was not among them. As the boys learned later, the town bully

32

had done his best to evade the draft, and had only registered when threatened with military action.

Then he made a virtue of necessity and talked big about having tried to volunteer in the air service, only to be refused. But most of those who heard Noddy Nixon talk understood him, and were not at all taken in.

"Where'd you fellows train?" asked Noddy, moving over toward his Cresville acquaintances.

"Camp Dixton," answered Ned. Then he added to Bob and Jerry: "Come on, fellows, I think our train's about to pull out."

None of the Motor Boys had any relish for talk with their former enemy. As for Noddy, he seemed to think he was doing them a favor by noticing them, and as they turned away he said:

"Camp Dixton isn't in it with Upyank, where our bunch was trained! We'll show you when we get to France!"

"I hope we don't run across him," murmured Jerry, as they got back to their seats, for Ned's alarm had proved true, and their train soon did pull out. Noddy and his crowd were a little later in starting from the junction, and then, as the Motor Boys were hauled on to their destination to embark for France, they discussed the past doings of the bully, and wondered how he would conduct himself in war.

From that they switched to the more pleasant topic of the recent visit of the girls, and speculated on what had become of Andy Rush.

"They might enlist him and let him talk some of the Huns to death," suggested Ned. "He could do that to perfection. But I'm afraid he's too small to get in the army."

"I wonder if we'll ever find the professor's two girls?" ventured Bob, meaning thereby Gladys Petersen and Dorothy Gibbs.

"I don't believe we'll have much time to look for them, if the fighting keeps up as fiercely as it has," and Jerry handed his chums a paper he had purchased, which gave a detailed account of some of the first fighting of the American Expeditionary Force, in the Toul sector, at Seicheprey. This fighting had taken place in April, and it was late in June when Ned, Bob and Jerry, with others from their camp, were on their way to France in that great movement of troops which was to prove the turning, and winning, point of the war. The account in the paper of the fighting at Seicheprey was a delayed one sent through the mail by a correspondent.

"Yes, it is getting hot," observed Ned. "But still we promised the professor we'd help him look for the girls."

"And so we shall, if we get the chance," declared Jerry. "I know what it would mean to the professor if he lost his half of the fortune and had to give up his work on the insects of the Amazon. Oh, we'll help him all right!"

Ned, Bob and Jerry on the Firing Line.   Page

The journey of the boys to the "Atlantic Seaport," as Hoboken and New York, as well as other well-known cities, were called in the newspapers during the war, was not eventful. Their train was one of many hundreds rushing troops to the transports, and in due time Ned, Bob and Jerry found themselves getting off at a big dock in Hoboken and going aboard a transport—a former German liner, her machinery rebuilt after the ship's German crew had done their best to disable it.

"Well, we're here!" announced Jerry, as he eased his pack from his shoulders to the deck, an example followed by Ned and Bob.

"Yes, we're here, and we'll soon be—there!" and Ned nodded in the direction of France—or where he thought it was.

Somewhere a band was playing. Thousands of soldiers were crowding on board, and there would be more thousands after them—a stream that would not end until Prussianism had been dealt its death-blow.

There was a period of seeming chaos while the troops were getting settled and disposing of their baggage. Then the three chums had a chance to look about them, and proceeding to the stern of the vessel they glanced across the Hudson to New York, where the towering buildings showed dimly through a harbor haze.

"Wonder when we'll see them again," remarked Jerry, in a low voice.

Neither of his chums answered. They were thinking, though.

Late that afternoon the preparation and bustle seemed redoubled. More soldiers and a number of officers came aboard, and then, suddenly, after bugles had blared and bells had clanged, there was a tremor through the big transport.

"We're off!" cried Bob.

"For France!" added Ned.

"And I'm glad to be with you!" said a voice behind Jerry, who, turning, beheld Professor Snodgrass.

CHAPTER VIII

THE TRAINING CAMP

My readers may well guess that Ned, Bob and Jerry were glad to see the scientist. He was like part of their "own folks," and though they had many friends among their army chums, and though they liked, and were liked, by their officers, our three heroes felt that with Professor Snodgrass along it was like taking part of Cresville aboard with them.

"So you got here all right, did you?" asked Ned with a smile, as he and the others shook hands with the scientist.

"Yes, I'm here; and I wish we were across. I dread the voyage."

"Submarines?" asked Jerry.

"Oh, no, I wasn't thinking of them," answered the professor. "But I am anxious to get across, not only to begin my study of the effect of war noises on European insects, but to search for those two young ladies. I have been reading considerable about war conditions in France and Germany since Professor Petersen made me his part heir, and I fear the young ladies may have a hard time."

"Yes, they are very likely to," assented Ned. "But until we get there we can't do anything to help them. However, we'll do our best for you and them when we do get there—if we have a chance—after getting a Hun or two," he added.

"That's right," said Mr. Snodgrass. "The winning of the war is the first consideration. I wish I were young enough to fight. But I have contributed to the Red Cross, to the Salvation Army, the Knights of Columbus and the Y. M. C. A. and the Y. W. C. A.; and I've mailed every magazine I finished reading and sent over all the books I could spare."

The boys winked at one another. They gave full credit to Professor Snodgrass for his contributions to the five organizations, which, with the Jewish Welfare League, did so much to help win the war.

"But if the boys in camp over there had to depend for reading on the dry, scientific magazines and books the professor sent them they'd be hard put," commented Jerry to his chums, afterward.

"Well, we're moving, anyhow," observed Bob, as he and the others noticed that tugs were backing the transport out into the river. "Now that we're under way, don't you think we'd better go and see about—"

"Grub!" finished Jerry, fairly taking the word out of Chunky's mouth.

The stout lad glared a moment, and then said:

"Well, yes, grub! Why not? We have to eat, don't we?"

"You said it, Bob!" exclaimed Ned. "Go to it!"

But the boys found they need not have worried about the matter of eating or sleeping. Competent hands had the comfort of the soldiers in charge and there was nothing lacking that could be obtained. They were taken in charge by officers, divided into squads, assigned to certain lifeboats, and told where to report when an alarm for a submarine attack, real or simulated, was sounded.

Professor Snodgrass told how he had secured permission to come aboard the transport with his friends, the young soldiers—no easy matter—and how he had been designated as a "correspondent," though Jerry Hopkins, on hearing this, remarked:

"I suppose if he did send any news it would be to the Bug Hunter's Review, describing the life of an insect on an army transport."

"Very likely," agreed Ned.

And so, amid the blaring whistle salutes of river craft, the former German liner dropped down the bay and started for France with the young soldiers who were to do their part in ending barbarous militarism forever.

It was not exactly a gay trip. There were many who were seasick in spite of the calm weather, and there was little to do on board. Only a few books were available to read, and these were in constant use. Aside from lifeboat drill there was little to occupy the boys.

But there was always the fear of a submarine attack when they should reach the infested zone, and the boys looked forward to this as something that would relieve the monotony.

There was a gun crew on the transport—several of them, in fact—and the troop ships were escorted by war vessels and the swift, snake-like destroyers, which moved with such remarkable speed.

One day, after the usual lifeboat drill, which was held at different hours each day so that none would suspect when it was coming, the three chums were standing near the forward gun, rather idly scanning the water. The night had been a dreary one, cooped up as they were in the darkness, for now that they were approaching the danger zone, all but the most necessary lights were dimmed.

Up above, and on various parts of the deck, were the lookouts, scanning with strained and eager eyes the expanse of water ahead of them for a sight of the white wake that would indicate a periscope, or, perchance, hoping to see the wet, glistening sides of a "steel fish" itself, as it broke water before sending the deadly torpedo.

"Well, boys, how goes it?" asked a voice behind the three chums, and they recognized Professor Snodgrass.

As Jerry turned to speak to him, having finished a remark in which he had speculated as to what had become of Noddy Nixon, who was not on board, one of the men cried:

"What's that?"

He pointed to a spot about two points off the port bow, and Ned, Bob and Jerry, as well as several others, distinctly saw a little commotion in the water.

"A sub, as sure as you're a foot high!" cried a marine, just as a bugle call to quarters was blown, for a lookout, too, had observed the disturbance in the water.

Instantly the gun crew was in action, and several shots were fired from the bow gun. The reports had hardly ceased echoing when some remarkable activity was displayed, not only aboard the transport, but on the part of the convoying squadron.

As the shells splashed into the sea near the spot where the commotion had been observed, there were smudges of black smoke at several points on either side of the troopship. These were the funnels of the destroyers belching out clouds of vapor that told of their approach under forced draught. And as the other guns on the transport awoke and began firing on the suspected submarine, up came racing the swift craft, the men on board eagerly looking for a target.

Then their big guns got into action, and for a time the sea in the vicinity of the suspected place was churned by exploding shells, while one destroyer, the fastest of the flotilla, shot right over the place where the lookout thought he had seen a periscope, and dropped two depth bombs that added further to the churning of Neptune's element.

Meanwhile, for the second occasion in a short time, lifeboat stations were sounded, and the soldiers, donning their life preservers, took their places to await what might follow—possibly, an order to abandon ship after she had been struck by a torpedo.

But this contingency did not arise. The destroyers swarmed around the transport, seeking in vain for something substantial on which to expend their ammunition, and then the scare was over.

And whether it was only a scare, or whether a real submarine had shown her periscope and then dived before sending a torpedo, could, of course, only be surmised. But no chances were being taken, and the transport on which the Cresville boys traveled was not the only one of the American Expeditionary Forces that believed itself the object of a frustrated attack.

"If that was a sub, it came out pretty far to meet us," observed Jerry, when the excitement had died away and they were at ease once more.

"No telling where they'll be found," said a noncommissioned officer. "If that had been one I believe we'd have got her, though."

"Surest thing you know!" declared Ned Slade emphatically.

This was the only incident that marked the passage. Of course, at various times, especially during the nights, the lookouts may have imagined they saw the wake of a periscope or a torpedo, but there was no general alarm.

And finally, after what really was a tiresome voyage, and one the end of which was welcomed by all, the transport docked at a certain port in France, and Ned, Bob and Jerry were able, with their water-weary comrades, to go ashore.

"Here at last!" murmured Jerry, as he and his chums sought their own company.

"And where are the Huns we're going to fight?" asked Bob, looking around at the strange scenes.

"Oh, we won't see them right away," returned Ned. "It'll be more training camp for ours for a while. But we'll see real fighting soon enough. Don't worry."

"It can't come any too soon for me, Buddy!" exclaimed a tall, Southern lad, with whom the Motor Boys had become chummy at Camp Dixton. "Lead me to it!"

But there was much to be done before this would occur. After the boys had disembarked they were inspected, roll was called, and then they were told to march to a designated depot, there to eat and be fitted out for a march to the French village where they were to be billeted until sent to a training camp.

Professor Snodgrass could not, of course, stay with the army boys, but he announced that he would follow them as closely as possible, and keep in communication with them. As soon as might be he would arrange to begin the search for the two missing girls.

Not all that Ned, Bob and Jerry had read of the gigantic work undertaken to fit out and maintain the American armies in France prepared them for what they saw. The port where the transport docked had been transformed. Great storehouses and warehouses were erected. Whole railway systems had been built, with the American locomotives replacing the diminutive French ones. And the French population and army representatives were as much surprised at the initiative and wonderful progress of the American forces as were the new recruits themselves.

"Say, we're going into this war with both feet!" exclaimed Jerry admiringly.

"That's the only way to do it," said Ned. "The harder we go at it the sooner it will be over."

They had their "chow," and even Bob admitted that it was "mighty good," and, as you know, he was a connoisseur.

Then, with their comrades, the three Motor Boys marched to the place where they were to spend the night before going to the training camp. This was a small French village, and its quaint beauty, unspoiled by the Germans, was very attractive to the sea-weary soldiers.

Ned, Bob and Jerry were billeted with five others at a French farmhouse, where they were given beds in the attic. The "beds" were only piles of clean straw, but the lads were delighted with them after their close bunks on the ship.

"I can roll over now without falling out," said Ned, with a sigh of comfort as he stretched out.

They drew their rations the following morning, and breakfasted most heartily, if not luxuriously, and were ready for what the day held for them. This was nothing else than a journey to their training camp, which, they learned, was some miles behind the front lines where the fighting was going on.

"But you'll be moved up as fast as it's possible to do so," said the officer who directed them. "The fighting's getting heavier and heavier."

And this was true, for about this time the d American Division was in position east of Rheims where, a little later, a great German attack was launched, and, as all the world now knows, was flung back with disaster to the Hun forces.

The railroad journey, from a point near their disembarkation port to their training camp, was not a very comfortable one, as the troops had to travel in cars that were used at times for horses. But every one was in good spirits, and little inconveniences were laughed at.

And finally, after three days, the welcome word was given to leave the trains and march to the camp. This was situated in a beautiful part of France— that is, it had been beautiful before the spoliation by the Huns, and there Ned, Bob and Jerry, with thousands of their comrades, prepared for the last phase of their training. Before them was the enemy.

"Well, here at last!" remarked Jerry, as he eased himself from his pack, and, with his two chums, stacked the guns together. "I wonder what happens first?"

"Suppose you come over and have some chocolate?" suggested a voice behind the boys, and, turning, they saw a pleasant-faced young man, whose hair, however, was gray. He wore a semi-military uniform, but a glance at his sleeve showed the red triangle, and the letters "Y. M. C. A." were not needed to tell his character.

"Come over and make yourselves at home," he went on. "You'll have time before you'll be called on to report."

"Thank you, we will," said Jerry. "Some chocolate would touch the spot."

"I've got two spots that need touching," laughed Bob.

"Won't you boys come, too?" invited the Y. M. C. A. worker, as he turned to some others who had marched up as Ned, Bob and Jerry were moving away.

"What? Trail in with a lot of psalm-singing goody-goodies?" was the sneering retort of one, and it needed only a glance to show that the speaker was Noddy Nixon.

"He's here—worse luck!" murmured Ned.

"No Y. M. C. A. for mine!" sneered Noddy.

"Boor!" muttered Bob, in protest.

"There is a Knights of Columbus station next to ours, and a Salvation Army hut, as well as a Jewish Community station, here in camp," was the gentle answer of the secretary. "If you prefer one of those you will be very welcome, I know. We are all working together for you boys."

"None for mine!" sneered Noddy. "I want some cigarettes!"

"I can let you have some at my foyer," said the secretary, with a smile. "I don't smoke myself, but I like the smell of it mighty well. Come along."

But Noddy laughed sneeringly, and would not go. However, Ned, Bob and Jerry accompanied the Y. M. C. A. man, and very glad they were to buy, at a modest price, some cups of chocolate, and also some cakes of it to put in their pockets.

"These Y. M. C. A. and K. C. places are all to the merry!" voted Ned. "They were great back at Camp Dixton, but they're twice as good here!"

"And we'll look after you, as well as we can, when you get on the firing line," said their new friend. "You'll have to depend on the Salvation Army lassies for doughnuts, but we can give you smokes and chocolate almost any time. Have some more!"

He made the boys and their comrades so welcome that they hated to leave to go to roll call. But this must be done, and soon they were assigned to barracks, much the same as in Camp Dixton.

CHAPTER IX

ON THE FIRING LINE

The training Ned, Bob and Jerry went through in the French camp, though on a more intense scale and with greater attention to detail, was much like that which they had obtained at Camp Dixton, and that has been related at length in the volume preceding this.

There were the same drills to go through, only they were harder, and in charge were men who had seen terrible fighting. Some of them were American army officers, sent back from the front to instruct the new recruits, and others were French and British officers, detailed to teach the raw troops who, at first, were brigaded with the veterans.

It was rise early in the morning, drill hard all day, attend some school of instruction in the evening, and then, after a brief visit perhaps to the Y. M. C. A. hut or one of the other rest tents, go to bed, to get up and do it all over again the next day.

But the boys never felt it monotonous, nor did they complain of the hard work. They knew it was necessary, and here on the very fighting ground itself—in wonderful France—there was a greater incentive to apply oneself to the mastering of the lessons of the war.

Then, too, they saw or heard at first hand of the indescribable cruelties and atrocities of the Huns. Ned, Bob, Jerry, and their comrades saw with what fervor the French and British were proceeding with the war, and their own spirits were inflamed.

No work was too hard for them, from learning to throw hand grenades, taught by men who had had them thrown at them, to digging trenches laid out after the fashion of those on either side of No Man's Land. Then came small sham engagements, when, imagining the sample trenches to be held by Germans, a company would storm them to drive out the "enemy."

In fair and rainy weather this work went on, and it rained more often than not, as Jerry wrote home to his mother. The chums could write, but there was no telling when the missives would be delivered, nor when they would get any in return, for there was such congestion that the mail service broke down at times, and no wonder. So, though eventually the home folks—and in them is included "the girls"—got all the mail intended for them, there were days of anxious waiting.

Meanwhile the Motor Boys were perfecting themselves as soldiers, and were winning the commendation of their officers. Jerry was promoted to be first corporal, and in his squad of seven were Ned and Bob, much to their delight.

"It's a pleasure to take orders from you, old man," said Ned.

"Well, I won't give any more than I have to," remarked the tall lad, now taller and more bronzed than ever.

Professor Snodgrass had managed to find quarters in a village not far from camp, and from there he came to see the boys occasionally. He was getting his affairs in shape to proceed with the study of the matter at present under his attention.

"Have you heard anything from Miss Petersen or Miss Gibbs?" asked Jerry.

"No, not a word," was the answer. "I have sent several letters, and made inquiries of the authorities here, but the latter give me very little encouragement. That's bad, too; for I've just had word from home that makes my share in that inheritance seem of more importance than ever," and the professor gave a little sigh.

"Why, what's happened, Professor?" questioned Jerry, with quick sympathy.

"I lent some money," explained Professor Snodgrass, "to one of my friends— an old friend with whom I went through college—to help him over a hard place. But he has not got over his troubles; in fact, his affairs are growing worse, and it looks as if I would never get my money back. And that will cripple me, cripple me badly, boys. Yes, I need the money that Professor Petersen was good enough to leave me."

"Well, let's hope that you find those girls quickly, Professor, and get that inheritance very soon," said Ned.

"But I am afraid I shall have to wait until you boys capture Germany, and then I can go in and search."

"Us boys—with help," chuckled Jerry.

"Well, if it keeps up the way we've started we'll soon have the Hun on the run!" declared Ned, and he spoke with some truth, for soon was to be the beginning of the successful American advance.

Greatly to their relief the boys saw little of Noddy Nixon, for he was housed in barracks at the opposite end of the camp from those in which they were billeted. But they met him occasionally, and listened with ill-concealed disgust to his boasts, and his talk of having tried in vain to enlist before he was drafted.

"If they'd give me an aeroplane I'd go over the German lines and make 'em sit up and take notice!" boasted the bully.

"Why don't you send home for what's left of your 'Tin Fly'?" asked Ned, with a wink at his chums.

"Aw, you dry up!" commanded Noddy, for this airship, which he had once built to compete in an exhibition, was a sore point with him, as it had not justified its name.

Meanwhile, all along the line in the sector where the American troops were stationed hard fighting was going on. On either flank were French and English forces, but the boys of Uncle Sam were holding up their end of the work exceedingly well.

"When can we get into it?" sighed Ned one evening, when reports came in of heavy fighting, during which certain American units had won distinction.

"Very soon, so I hear," returned Jerry. "Our intensive training is nearly over. We may be moved up to the front any day now."

"The sooner the quicker," cried Bob. "Maybe the eats won't be so good farther front, but we'll see some action!"

Of course, there had been "action" in plenty at camp, but it was of the safe variety, and this did not appeal to the boys.

Then their chance came. One morning after drill emotion, like electricity, seemed to run through the camp.

"What's up?" came the queries from all sides.

"We're ordered to the firing line!" was the answer.

And then came cheers! Cheers that showed of what stuff America's fighters were made.

The news proved true. That evening, under the cover of darkness, so that no lurking Hun planes might detect the movement, a considerable body of troops from the training camp was sent up toward the front, to relieve some battle-scarred units.

At first, as the three chums and their comrades marched along, there was joking and laughing. Then this died away. The seriousness of the situation began to be comprehended. It was not that any one was afraid. The boys were realizing the gravity of the occasion, that was all.

"Hark! what's that?" asked Bob, as he marched along with Ned, Jerry, as corporal, being file leader. "Is it thunder?"

They stepped lightly so as to listen more intently.

"The guns!" explained a lieutenant hurrying past. "Those are the guns on the firing line you hear. There must be a night attack."

The guns of the front! Fighting was actually very near, for, though the boys in camp had often heard a distant rumble when there was a big bombardment on, this was the first time they had heard so plainly the hostile guns. It gave them a thrill, even as they felt the ground tremble beneath them.

And so, in the darkness, they moved up to their new camp—a camp on the very edge of the fighting; and from where they came to a halt, to wait for morning before being assigned to the trenches, they could see the lurid fires that flared across No Man's Land.

Tired and weary, but with an eagerness nothing could subdue, the chums and their comrades awoke the next morning as the bugle called them. At first they could not realize where they were, and then with a rush it came to them.

"On the firing line!" cried Jerry. "Just where we wanted to be! Now for some action!"

Hardly had he spoken when there sounded a terrific explosion, and the boys were fairly blown off their feet, toppling to the ground.

There was action for them!

CHAPTER X

IN THE TRENCHES

Stunned and bruised, the three chums and several of their comrades around them were incapable of action for a little while. Then, as Jerry raised himself from the ground, he heard Bob ask:

"What hit us, anyway? Are the Germans attacking?"

"Gee!" was Bob's muttered protest.

"Get up!" some one cried. "You're all right. It was a bomb from a Hun plane, but it missed its mark."

"Seems to have hit me all right," observed Ned, whose face was bleeding, though only from scratches.

"You were knocked down by the concussion," explained the officer who had told them to get up. "It was a close call all right, but no one is hurt. Fall in for roll call!"

Ned, Bob, Jerry, and some of the other soldiers scrambled to their feet. They had been on the point of answering roll call when the explosion came, and now that the danger was over, at least for the time being, they had a chance to see what had caused it.

The aeroplane from which the bomb had been dropped was not now in sight, but this is what had happened. One of the German machines passing over the front line, as they often did, had escaped the Allied craft, and had also managed to pass through the firing of the anti-aircraft guns. Whether the machine had gone some distance back, hoping to drop bombs on an ammunition dump, or whether it came over merely to take a pot shot at the American trenches, was never known.

But the aviator had dropped a large explosive bomb, which, luckily for the Motor Boys and their comrades, had fallen into an open space, though not far from one of the camouflaged stations where the soldiers were quartered before being taken up to the front-line trenches. The explosion had blown a big hole in the ground and damaged some food stores, but that was all, except that when the Americans were about to answer roll call they were knocked down by the concussion, and some, like Ned, were scratched and cut by flying dirt and stones, or perhaps by fragments of the bursting bomb.

"See, no one is hurt," went on the officer, as if to reassure those who were soon to take their places in the front-line trenches. "Good luck was with you that time."

"I hope it keeps up," murmured Bob. "It's a mean trick to shoot a man before he has his breakfast," and then he wondered why the others laughed.

They all looked curiously, and it may be said, thankfully, at the big hole made by the bomb. As the officer had said, only good luck had prevented some of the boys from filling that hole.

After this Jerry was silent and thoughtful.

"Well, what's next?" asked Ned, after an examination had shown that his wounds were merely scratches, for which he refused to go to the hospital, or even a dressing station.

"Breakfast, I hope," said Bob, and this it proved to be.

The excitement caused by the dropping of the bomb soon died away, though Ned, Bob, Jerry, and some of the other soldiers who had not yet been under hostile fire, felt their nerves a bit unsteady for some time.

But the veterans, of whom there were many, appeared to take it as a matter of course. It had happened before, they said, and probably would again.

"But that's what we came here for—war," remarked Jerry, as he and his chums finished their breakfast—no very elaborate meal, and one to which little time was given. "We've got to take our chances."

Up and down the line, on either side of the sector where the three chums were to receive their baptism of fire, already begun, could be heard dull booming. It was the firing of heavy guns, and might indicate an attack in progress or one being repelled by either side. Here the Allied and German lines were close together, in some places the front-line trenches being less than six hundred feet apart. Between was the famed and terrible No Man's Land.

"I wonder if Professor Snodgrass will ever get up as far as this," mused Ned, as they prepared to go back to their quarters and begin the day's business.

"The firing wouldn't keep him away, if he thought he could find some bugs," answered Jerry. "And if he wants to ascertain the effect of noises on crickets all he has to do is to bring the crickets here. We can supply the noise."

"I should say so!" agreed Bob. "It's getting worse, too! Listen to that!"

Indeed, with the broadening of day the noise of the big and small guns increased. Whether a great battle was impending or merely local engagements, the boys had no means of knowing.

The position to which they had been brought, and where they would spend about a week, holding the front and supporting line trenches, until relieved by a new command, ran up and over a little wooded hill. From this vantage point, which had more than once been stormed in vain by the Germans, could be seen the country beyond No Man's Land—a portion of France held by the enemy. And in the brief glimpse the Motor Boys had of it, smoke-covered and stabbed with flashes of fire here and there as it was, they saw something of what war meant.

"The professor is going to have some job on his hands if he expects to find any young ladies on the other side of that," and Ned waved his hand to indicate the terrain possessed by the Huns.

"Oh, we can get through if we attack in force," declared Bob. "And maybe that's why they brought us up—there may be going to be an attack."

"We'll have to get through—for objects big and little; that the professor may find his girls and his inheritance and," and here Ned's lips set a little grimly, "that we may help to bring back freedom to the earth."

"There may be an attack all right, if Foch, Pershing and the other generals think it's a good time for it," said Jerry. "But as for having it postponed until our arrival, well, you boys have some ideas of your ability."

"Oh, I didn't mean that!" cried Bob. "I meant that maybe we'd be in the big battle."

"I hope we are," said Ned. "We want to do our share."

This opportunity soon came to the boys. As soon as they reached their headquarters—a series of ruined buildings in which they had passed the night—they were told to get ready to go up and take their places in the trenches. But first they were given a little talk by one of the officers, who explained the necessity of donning gas masks at the first alarm. Other instructions were given, and then, when it was seen that every man had everything he needed, from the first-aid kit to the grotesque-looking gas mask, the trip to the first-line trenches was begun.

So much has been written about the World War that it seems needless to explain anything about the trenches. As all know, they were a series of ditches, about six feet deep, dug along in front of similar ditches constructed by the enemy. The distance between the two lines of trenches varied from a few hundred feet to several thousand.

The ditches, or trenches, were not in straight rows. They zig-zagged to make attacks on them more difficult. There were several rows of trenches on both sides of No Man's Land. This was so that in the event of an attack the men could fall back from one line of trenches to the other, fighting meanwhile to drive off the enemy.

The trenches were narrow, about wide enough for one man, though two might pass by squeezing. At intervals, however, were wider places where food or wound-dressing emergency stations could be established. At other places there were large excavations where dugouts were constructed, and there relief parties rested and slept if they could between periods of duty.

The bottoms of some of the trenches were covered with "duck boards," or short planks, with spaces between to let the water run out, and in certain parts of France it seemed to some of the boys to rain about three hundred out of the three hundred and sixty-five days of the year.

The trenches were sometimes braced with boards and cross pieces of wood, such as is often used when a sewer is dug through the streets, and again wicker-work, or jute bagging, might be used to hold the earth firm.

Below the top of the trenches, in certain places, were projections. These were firing steps, and the men stepped up on these to aim their rifles at the enemy. In certain other places were set up improvised periscopes, so that an officer could look "over the top," and, by a series of reflecting mirrors, observe what was going on in the enemy's country.

Again, at other places in the trenches, light artillery, such as machine guns and grenade throwers were set up. Here and there were little stoves to warm the food brought up whenever a relief party could get through the rain of shells. In some places heavy concrete or wooden dugouts were constructed, well under ground, though the Germans did more of this than the Allies, the Hun trenches being very elaborate at times.

And it was to these trenches that Ned, Bob and Jerry, with their comrades, were led. There they would remain on duty for a specified time differing under varying conditions, or until an attack was either made by them or by the enemy. After that, in case the enemy were successful, trenches farther in the rear must be occupied. But in the event of the German attack being repulsed, and a counter-attack carrying the Allies forward, advanced trenches—possibly those deserted by the Huns—would be used.

"Forward!" came the command, and the three Motor Boys advanced. They did not march long in open formation. To do this would be dangerous, within range of the German guns as they were, and, too, they might be seen by a Hun observer in an aeroplane. So, in a little while the advancing squad, of which Ned, Bob and Jerry formed a part, found itself in a communicating trench. This was a ditch dug at right-angles to the front-line trenches, and through this the relief passed, and food and ammunition were brought up.

The communicating trench zig-zagged, as did the front-line ones, to provide greater safety, and the boys finally gave up trying to guess in which direction they were going. All they could see was the sky above their heads.

Suddenly, however, the trench widened, and they saw another crossing it. At this point, too, there was what seemed to be a rough door, made of planks nailed together.

"This is your dugout," said the leading officer, indicating that Ned, Bob and Jerry, with some others, were to remain there, while he led the rest farther on.

"Glad you've come," remarked a haggard-looking officer, who was to be relieved by the commander of the squad in which were the three chums.

"Has Fritz been bothering you?" asked Lieutenant Anderson, who was in charge of the relief.

"Has he? Well, rather! And then some! You have my permission to stay as long as you please! Come on, boys!" and he led his war-weary men back to a rest billet.

"Make yourselves at home, fellows," said the lieutenant. "And wipe your feet before you come in," he added with a laugh, as he looked down at his muddy boots.

The passwords had been given and received. The other relief party had passed on to allow other worn-out men to get some rest. Ned, Bob and Jerry looked about them. They were in a dirt ditch, filled here and there with puddles of water from the last rain, and the clouds still hung in the sky.

"Where are the German trenches?" asked Ned.

"Where? Right in front of us—over there," and the lieutenant pointed. "Wait, I'll show you, and everybody get this, and take a lesson from it!" he added.

He held up a steel helmet on the end of a stick. In an instant it went spinning off and fell at his feet in the trench. He picked it up, pointing grimly to a neat little hole through it and said:

"That's what will happen to any one of you if he sticks his head up. You're in the front-line trench. Don't forget it!"

CHAPTER XI

A NIGHT PATROL

Every one who saw the heavy steel hat so neatly pierced by the swift bullet was impressed by the object lesson, as the lieutenant had intended all of them should be. But, somehow or other, Bob Baker seemed more fascinated than either of his chums, and, indeed, more than any other member of that particular relief squad.

"Did a Hun bullet do that?" asked Bob, as he picked up the head protector and looked at the hole.

"That's what it did, my boy," answered the officer. "And that's what will happen to you, or any one else, if you stick your head up above the trench."

"And the Huns did that!" murmured Bob, who seemed not to be able to efface from his mind the picture of the punctured, spinning helmet. "Then we're right within range of their fire."

"Considerably so," answered the lieutenant. "In places the German trenches are only six hundred feet away, and that's nothing for the modern rifle. It can kill at over a mile."

"So, Chunky," observed Jerry, "you've been under fire now."

"Yes," said Bob, and his voice was sober, "we've been under fire."

"Of course this isn't anything!" the lieutenant exclaimed with a laugh, as he kicked aside the bullet-punctured helmet Bob had dropped. "This is just a little byplay. You'll be under heavier fire than this, but don't worry. It takes a good many bullets to get a man. However, don't think of that. Do your duty. That's what you're here for!"

The lieutenant looked somewhat anxiously into the faces of the relief squad he was to command. Every officer likes to know that he has the bravest of men in the army, and this young officer was no exception. The firing line where the Motor Boys now were—the front-line trenches—was no place for cowards.

But the faces that looked back into the young lieutenant's gave no reflection of fear. And at this he breathed in relief. There was puzzled wonder on the countenance of some, and grim determination on others, and this last was what counted.

And then began for the Motor Boys and their chums a life of the utmost tension, strenuousness, and danger, although theirs was a comparatively quiet sector at that particular stage of the war, and they were holding the trenches more to guard against a surprise attack than anything else.

51

"Well, there's one comfort," remarked Jerry, as he was placed in his station in the trench, with Bob on one side and Ned on the other, both within talking distance.

"What?" asked Bob. "Do we get better eats here?"

"Eats, you heathen!" exclaimed Ned. "Can't you forget that once in a while? What are you going to do if the Germans make you a prisoner? They won't feed you at all!"

"Then I won't be a prisoner!" declared Bob. "But what were you going to say about comfort, Jerry?"

"We don't have to drill," was the answer.

And this was true. All the life of the camp was now done away with, even the training camp of France, where the boys had finished their war education, so to speak. But if they did not have to drill there was plenty else to occupy them.

While on duty in the trench they had constantly to be on the alert, and this not to guard against the unexpected approach of some friendly officer, bent on determining how his sentries were performing their duty, but to be on the watch against the approach of a deadly enemy. There must be no sleeping— not even dozing—on post.

Then, too, there was work to do. There was food and water to bring up, and fire wood to scurry for when the chance offered, for it was not often possible to bring up hot rations to the front lines, and the boys heated their own as best they could, in discarded tin cans with a few twigs for fuel.

There were lines of trenches to cut, dugouts to repair after they had been blown to bits by the German guns, and there was barbed wire to replace under cover of darkness when it had been severed by the rain of steel and lead from the enemy's guns.

So the three chums and their comrades found no lack of things to keep them busy in the trenches. They had their hours off, of course, when they were permitted to go back to the dugout, and there, in comparative safety, they might try to sleep. This was not easy, for though in a manner they became used to the constant roaring and blasting of the big guns, there was always an under-current of disturbances of other kinds. They were on the firing line, and the enemy did not let them forget it.

Every day the aeroplanes went over the lines, and more than once there was a battle in mid-air above where Ned, Bob and Jerry were on duty. Once a Hun plane came down in flames, so near they could hear the thud as it struck.

At times, after a period of comparative quiet, the trenches on both sides of No Man's Land would suddenly awaken into life. This would be caused by a fear, either on the part of the Germans or the troops from America, that one or the other was starting a raid. Then the machine guns would open fire, they would be augmented by the rifles of the men, and, if the shooting kept up long enough, the rival batteries would awaken and the big guns would speak.

It was one day, when the three chums had been on duty in the front-line trench about a week, that, as they were talking about the chance of seeing Professor Snodgrass and helping him in his search for the two girls, something spun past Ned's head with a whine, and, with a vicious ping, imbedded itself in the trench wall behind him.

"What's that?" exclaimed Bob.

"That sniper again," answered Ned. "That's the closest he's come. We'd better move, fellows, or he may get one of us."

"A sniper!" exclaimed Jerry. "Has he been taking pot shots at you?"

"Several of 'em. I've tried to get him, but I can't figure out where he hides. Better move down the trench a bit. He seems to train his gun on this particular spot."

"Gee!" gasped Bob.

Bob and Jerry had moved up from their own stations to where Ned was placed, as it was a quiet period of the day, and it was while they were talking that the shot came.

"I'd like to have a try at him," said Jerry. "It's queer he can send a bullet down into this trench. It must come from above. A shot from the German trenches wouldn't reach here over the top, unless it was fired up, and landed here as it came down."

"Then it would be a spent ball," argued Bob, "and it wouldn't sing out the way that one did."

"You're right," agreed Ned. "It was fired from above—you can tell that by the slant it took as it came in. But it didn't come from an aeroplane. There hasn't been any over the trench for a long while. No, it's some German sniper, and he's out there in the woods, I believe. Up a tree, most likely, where he can fire down into our trench. He must have a long-range rifle."

"We ought to try to get him," argued Jerry. "Have you, Ned?"

"Yes, I've tried to bait him, so I could find out where he shoots from and nip him in return, but I haven't been able to."

"Then I'm going to have a shot at him," declared Jerry, who was rated as an expert in the use of the rifle, as his badge showed.

But his plan of getting revenge on the Hun, who had so nearly shot Ned, was not destined to be carried out at once. For just then the relief of the boys came up, and they were marched back to the dugout for a rest period.

It was after they had enjoyed this, and were counting on again doing their turn in the trenches that their chance came to go out on night patrol, one of the most dangerous missions in the line of duty.

So far, since the Motor Boys had come up to the firing line, there had been no really serious fighting in their immediate sector. On either side of them there had been skirmishes, but a mile or so away, so they had had no chance to participate. Also there had been night raids, but Ned, Bob and Jerry had not been in them.

This does not mean that Ned, Bob and Jerry were in no danger, for, as has been shown, a bullet came near ending Ned's career. And aside from this, there had been bombs dropped near them from Hun aeroplanes, and once a whole portion of the trench, just beyond where they were stationed, had been caved in by a shell from a German gun, and several brave lads had been killed, while others were terribly injured. But Ned, Bob and Jerry had come out unscathed.

Also there had been waves of gas—the ordinary chlorine gas, and again the more dangerous mustard variety. In fact, the Germans used their yellow-cross and their green-cross gases alternately against the sector where the Cresville chums were. But prompt use of the protective masks prevented any casualties.

So, as has been said, when the three chums were resting in the dugout, wondering what their next duty would be, an officer came in, and, when he had returned the salutes, he said:

"Volunteers are wanted for a raiding party to-night. There's a German dugout not far away, and the commander thinks we have a good chance to get some prisoners and thus learn a thing or two about what Fritz is up to in this section. There's also a chance, as I needn't mention, that none of us will come back. Now then, who wants to go?"

There was a moment of hesitation, and then, to the credit of the young soldiers, every one stepped forward.

"Um!" mused the officer. "I can't use you all. Thank you, just the same. Now let's see," and he proceeded to pick out his squad.

To their delight Ned, Bob and Jerry were selected, and at once began to prepare for the dangerous mission. None of them gave more than a passing thought to the reflection that all might safely return or none of them come back.

CHAPTER XII

BOB IS MISSING

Careful preparations had been made for this night raid. It was the constant effort of both sides, during the period of trench fighting, to get possession of facts which would allow successful attacks to be carried out later. And to do this it was needful to get close to the enemy's line. By so doing, certain things might be overheard in the talk among the soldiers, or (for the results of the listening were uncertain) better still, was the capture of prisoners. Once they were taken back of the lines, questioned and searched, much of value might be obtained.

This, as a matter of fact, worked much better for the Americans than it did for the Germans. If the Huns did succeed in capturing, during a raid, some of our boys, they got little information from them about the units with which the boys of Uncle Sam were connected. Nor did the Huns learn much as to the strength of the forces opposed to them, except, perhaps, in the way of exaggeration.

"The American captive is more inclined to utter the equivalent of 'nothing doing,'" remarked Jerry, one day when discussing the matter.

On the other hand, the German prisoners captured, almost invariably, were glad that their fate had thus been ordered. They were sure of decent treatment, they were in no more danger of being killed and, more than anything else, they would be better fed than in their own trenches.

So it is no wonder they gave valuable information under the skilful questioning of the American officers. Still this information had to be carefully checked up before being acted on, as it would not do to run into danger as a result of what some Hun captive told.

"We are going out to try our luck," explained the lieutenant who was to lead Ned, Bob, Jerry, and their comrades, numbering half a score, out on a night raid. "There's a German dugout not far from here, and near by a machine-gun nest, and if we can get close enough to rush it, and capture those we don't kill, we may make it possible for a big forward movement—if the information we get is of the right sort. So get ready. Gas masks, hand grenades—rifles will be in the way—automatic pistols, of course, and don't forget to blacken your faces."

This precaution was always taken by night raiding parties. The Germans adopted the habit of sending up illuminating devices, known as "star shells," at frequent intervals over No Man's Land. This was to guard against a party of the enemy advancing on the trenches. The shells gave a very bright light, and nothing stands out more conspicuously in such a glare than a white face. So it was the custom to blacken countenances and hands when a night-raiding party went over the top.

It was not without a little feeling of nervousness and apprehension that the three friends and their chums made their preparations. But it was an apprehension of failure rather than fear. They wanted to succeed, to get results, and they were afraid they might fail. They were not afraid, personally. Still they were taking big chances, and they all knew it.

"Ought we to leave some word for Professor Snodgrass?" asked Ned, as he and his friends were making ready about midnight.

"Word about what?" Jerry inquired.

"Well, in case we don't come back we can't help him in his search, as we promised."

"If we don't come back our friends will know it, and they can tell the professor if he inquires for us," said Jerry grimly. "Let it go at that. If we get back we'll be here ourselves in case the professor ever gets this far to the front. If we don't get back—well, he'll have to get some one else to help him. Come on!"

The last word was given, the final preparations had been made. Then silently, like shadows of the night, the figures crept out of the trench in the darkness and advanced toward the German lines.

The American barbed wire had been cut in places to let the party through. To pass the German barrier they would have to do their own cutting, and they were provided with tools for this purpose.

Silently they went down the lane of wire, now and then passing grim sentries to whom the password was given. And then, coming to the gap in the wire, Ned, Bob and Jerry, with the others, passed through. Each member of the party carried an automatic pistol and several hand grenades. These were small, hollow containers, of cast-iron, loaded with a powerful explosive, which was set off after a certain trigger or spring or firing pin (according to the type used) was released by the thrower. The explosive blew the grenade to bits, and it was scored, or crisscrossed, by deep indentations so that the iron would break up into small pieces like shrapnel. The grenades could be carried in a pouch or in the pocket, and were harmless as long as the detonating device was not disturbed.

Silently the lieutenant led his men forward. Jerry Hopkins, the only noncommissioned officer in the squad, marched next, as in the event of the lieutenant being killed the command would fall to him.

No talking was permitted, and each man knew what he was to do, so no orders were necessary. On and on they went, and presently they found themselves traveling over the battle-scarred and shell-pitted territory of No Man's Land. They had got close to the German barbed wire when suddenly, as though their movements had been watched, several star shells were sent up by the Huns.

Instantly every man in the party fell flat on his face and did not move. It was the only thing to do. They resembled, as nearly as they might, the dead which lay all about them on the desolate field.

And some of the dead had been there a long time, as it was impossible for either side to bury them, though occasionally, at night, parties went out to bring in those in whom it was hoped a spark of life still remained.

Jerry found that he had thrown himself down close beside a dead Hun. He wanted desperately to move, for his position was grimly unpleasant, but he did not dare. This was not the most glorious side of war, but it was vitally necessary.

However, thanks to the precaution of blackened faces and hands, and to the dark uniforms, the party of night-raiders must have resembled the dead all about them, for no firing followed the illumination of star shells.

Then, when it was dark again, the party rose and went on. Good luck attended them thus far, in that they reached the German barbed wire undiscovered. Then began the ticklish work of cutting it, and in this there was much danger.

For some of the wire was under great tension, and, when cut, made a twanging sound like a broken harp or piano string. And this sound carried far in the silence of that sector. Other sectors were not so quiet, for firing was going on along both lines of trenches, though what movement was under way the Motor Boys did not know.

The sound of the wire as it was cut was deadened as much as possible by having a man hold the strand on either side of the place to be cut. This helped some, but not always, as the wire twisted itself from the grips of the soldiers, and sometimes the barbs injured them.

"All cut, Lieutenant," reported Jerry, as the final strand was severed. The commanding officer had been on watchful patrol while this was being done.

"Good!" was the low-voiced answer. "Come on, now. Every man with a grenade in either hand!"

Once more the party went forward. They were past the first German barbed wire now, but the way was still not completely open, for more opposing strands were found farther on. However, this was not unexpected, for often three or more lines of this American invention were to be found opposing the American forces.

Once more the cutters were called into play, and as the last strand was severed a dog, somewhere within the Hun lines, barked. Instantly all in the raiding party crouched down, for a burst of star shells might follow immediately.

However, the dog must have been believed to be a false alarmist, or else he was barking at some other disturbance than that caused by the raiders, for darkness still reigned.

Then, after waiting a moment to make sure all was right, the lieutenant led his men forward. So far they had not been challenged by the enemy, but now this immunity was to end, for when they had passed the final wire barrier and were advancing with tense steps toward the German dugout, with grenades in readiness, there came a sharp, guttural order to halt.

It was in the German tongue, as they all knew, and they all realized that the crucial moment had come.

The lieutenant, seeing a figure in the darkness before him, shot at it pointblank with his pistol. There was a murmured exclamation, and the sentry went down, his finger pressing the trigger of his rifle, discharging it as he fell dead.

"Come on now, boys! Give it to 'em!" cried the officer.

"Forward!" shouted Jerry Hopkins, and with Ned and Bob at his heels he rushed ahead, the others stumbling after him. They had reached the German trenches, and from them now poured several defenders. The main body were in the dugout a little farther on, and it was desired to attack this, and, if possible, capture some prisoners.

"Come on! Come on! Down with the Huns!" cried the lieutenant, and his battle yell was echoed by Jerry and the others.

Then began a fight in the dark, the details of which were never very clear to the Motor Boys. Bob said he let loose all the grenades he had at the advancing party of Germans and then rushed at them, head down, as though advancing the ball for a touchdown.

Ned declared that he fired his automatic pistol until he realized that it was empty, and then, throwing it away, thought for the first time of the grenades he carried. Then he began using them.

There was a deafening noise as the grenades of the Americans exploded in the faces of the advancing Huns, and they, in turn, threw hand bombs and opened fire with their rifles. The attack awoke to life sentries and guard parties all along the line, and the scene was illuminated by a burst of star shells.

"Come on! Into the trenches! They can't see us there so well!" yelled Jerry.

"That's the idea!" commanded the lieutenant. "Get to the dugout!"

So desperate and sudden had been the attack of the Americans that, after the first resistance, the Germans gave way and ran back, jumping down into the trenches whence they had come.

The raiding party asked nothing better than to follow, and for a time pursued the Huns along their own trenches, the bursting star shells above giving light enough to see.

"Are you there—Ned—Bob?" demanded Jerry, as he ran on, following the tortuous line of the trench.

"I'm here!" answered Ned.

"So'm I," added Bob. "Haven't a shot left, though."

"Here, take these," and Jerry handed over some spare grenades he had in a pouch slung at his back. "Don't pot any of our men, though. Some are ahead of us."

On ran the Motor Boys, and in another moment they came to the dugout—a pretentious affair of concrete, now well lighted, for the alarm of the attack had spread.

One of the raiding party threw a hand grenade inside the structure. There was a powerful explosion, not enough, indeed, to wreck the stout place, but sufficient to send the inmates scurrying out—what were left of them.

"Kamerad! Kamerad!" some of the wounded ones cried, and others held up their hands.

"Come on!" shouted the lieutenant. "Gather 'em in and let's get back. This place is getting too hot for us."

He spoke with truth, for on all sides the big guns were now beginning to bark, and a general engagement might be precipitated.

Some of the Americans snatched guns from the now cowed Germans, and prodded them back along the trench with the points of the bayonets. Others held hand grenades or automatic pistols ready, and the order to retreat was given.

Half a dozen Hun prisoners had been captured, but at a price, for when the lieutenant, hurrying his men back across No Man's Land, began to look over his party, he found three were missing. They had either been killed or wounded, or were left prisoners in the trenches.

"Are you there, boys?" asked Jerry again, of his chums, and he received reassuring answers from both.

"Hurt?" was his next inquiry, as they raced across the stretch, stopping every time there was a burst of star shells, and crouching down, making their prisoners do the same, to take shelter in some shell holes, some half-filled with water and others containing dead bodies.

"I'm all right," Bob answered. "Only a bit scratched by some Hun's bayonet, I guess."

"A bullet or a bayonet touched me in the side," came from Ned. "It's bleeding a bit, but not much. I'm all right."

Some of the others who were able to come back were not so fortunate, however, and two died later of wounds received in that night raid.

But the main party succeeded in getting back to the American lines, and hurried through the opening in the barbed wire, where a relief or a rescue party, whichever might be required, was in waiting.

"Good work!" commended the captain to his lieutenant. "And you got some prisoners?"

"Six!"

"That's fine. Couldn't be better. Get down now, there may be a Hun barrage in a minute. They'll be ripping mad when they find out what's happened. This was one of their main posts, and Prussians were on guard."

Jerry and Ned were each guarding a Hun prisoner, making him walk along ahead with upraised hands, while the guns, taken away from the Germans themselves, served as compelling weapons.

Into the trenches they had left a short time before the raiders made their way, and went to the dugout where they were to report. There the commanding officer of that sector met them.

Coming into the comparatively well-lighted place from the darkness, Jerry blinked as he looked at the captured Germans and then glanced to see how badly Ned was hurt.

He saw that his chum was pale, and noted blood on his hands, but Ned smiled in a reassuring way. Then, for the first time, Jerry noticed that Bob was not with them.

"Where's Chunky?" he demanded.

"Who?" asked the lieutenant. "I thought we only left Black, Jones, and Porter behind. Is there another missing?"

"Bob Baker, sir," answered Jerry. "But he was with us when we got back within our own wire. I was talking to him."

"Send out a searching party!" ordered the captain. "It is possible he was hit and didn't say anything about it, or a stray bullet may have found him after he reached our lines. Send out and see!"

CHAPTER XIII

"JUST LIKE HIM!"

Jerry and Ned both confessed, afterward, that the sinking feeling, which seemed to carry their hearts away down into their muddy shoes, was greater at the knowledge that Bob was missing than it had been when they set out in the darkness to raid the Germans across the desolate stretch of No Man's Land.

It was all so unexpected. He had gone through the baptism of fire with them—he had helped capture the Huns—and had been, seemingly, all right on the return trip. And then, on the very threshold of his own army home, so to speak, he had disappeared.

"Did any one see him fall or hear of his being hit?" asked the lieutenant, as he prepared to lead out a searching party. Ned and Jerry, of course, and by rights, would be members of it.

"No, he was right near me, Sir, and he said particularly, when I asked him, that he was only scratched," declared Jerry. "I made sure Ned was the worst hurt."

"How much are you hurt?" asked the captain, turning to Jerry's chum.

"Oh, it's only a scratch, Sir," was the quick answer. "I can't feel it now."

Ned did not speak the exact truth, but he did not want to be kept back from the search.

"Very well," said the captain. "You may go, but don't go too far. Much as we would like to find Baker we must not take too many chances and endanger this whole post. Be as quick as you can."

With their hearts torn between a desire for vengeance and apprehension, Ned and Jerry went out with the others. The riot started by the raid had quieted down, and it was possible for the searchers to advance above their own trenches without drawing the German fire.

First the sentries who had been on duty near the gap in the American wire were questioned. They had seen the party depart and come back, but they had not noticed any member of it fall as though wounded, and they were positive no Germans had been able to get near enough to capture Private Baker.

"But what can have happened to him?" asked the lieutenant.

"He may have been wounded internally, and didn't speak of it, Sir," suggested Ned, whose own wound was troubling him woefully. "Then he may have become so weak that he fell in the trench somewhere without a sound."

"That is possible. We must make a careful search."

This was done with pocket flashlights, for any general illumination would have, perhaps, drawn a German attack. But no sign of Bob was revealed. It was most mysterious, how he could disappear so suddenly and completely. Of course, in the general confusion, much more than this might have happened and not been noticed. But unless he had gone back after speaking to Jerry, he must either have fallen well within the American lines or have been captured there. And the last did not seem possible.

"Well," said the lieutenant, "we'll have to go over in No Man's Land and take a chance there. He must have gone back after something, and been potted. I'll have to go back and report and—"

He paused to listen. The tramp of approaching feet could be heard along the trench. Every man stood at attention, for it was possible that the enemy had slipped in between sentries and were going to pay a return visit.

But a moment later the murmur of voices was heard—voices that were unmistakably American. Some one asked:

"Is your squad stationed here?"

"About here, yes, Sir," was the answer, coming out of the darkness.

"It's Chunky!" cried Jerry.

"That's Bob!" added Ned, joyously.

And a moment later there came into the dim light of the flashlights the stout chum himself, escorted by three soldiers. He seemed to be all right, and he carried something that was not a grenade, in one hand.

"Where have you been, Chunky?" demanded Jerry. "We've been looking everywhere for you."

"Yes," added the lieutenant, "will you please explain why you did not report back with the rest of us?"

Bob seemed a trifle surprised at the rather stern order, but he smiled and answered:

"Why, I thought, as long as we got back all right, I was relieved from duty, so I went to get something to eat."

"Something to eat!" exclaimed the lieutenant.

"Something to eat," calmly repeated Bob. "You see it was this way. I was terribly hungry—"

"Nothing unusual," murmured Jerry, but the stout lad, paying no attention to the interruption, went on:

"So when I got back with the rest, after we captured the Huns, I smelled something cooking farther up in our trenches. I knew some of the fellows on duty there, and I felt sure they'd give me something to eat. It was liberty links they were cooking, sir, and—"

"Liberty links!" interrupted the lieutenant. "What are those?"

"They used to be called Frankfurters," explained Bob with a grin; "but since the war that's too German. So I went to get some liberty links, and I got 'em!" he added with a sigh of satisfaction.

"Well! Well!" exclaimed the lieutenant. And then, as he thought of what Bob and the others had gone through with that night, he had not the heart to add more.

"I only meant to run up in a hurry to where they were cooking 'em," explained Bob, "and come back with some for my bunkies. But I got to talking and eating—"

"Mostly eating," murmured Jerry.

"And then I forgot to come back," finished Bob.

"We told him he'd better report, Sir," said one of the escorting party. "He was with our bunch all right, and when he told us he'd been out with the night raiders and had slipped off before reporting back, we told him he'd better report. So we showed him the way, as the trenches are sort of mixed up around here."

"Very well," said the lieutenant, trying not to smile. "You may go back to your posts. Everything is explained."

And so Bob was restored to his company again, and in view of the successful raid no reprimand was given him. The capture of the German prisoners proved important, as information was obtained that proved of the greatest value afterward.

Ned's wound turned out to be only a flesh one, but it was painful enough, and kept him in the hospital a week. He would have fretted over thus being kept away while Bob and Jerry were fighting, but, as a matter of fact, his two chums received a rest period at this time, and so were out of the trenches the same time that Ned was.

But the war was far from won, and every man possible was needed on the firing line, so that, in due season, the three chums found themselves back again. And under no very pleasant circumstances.

For it rained and rained, and then rained some more, though Jerry insisted that where they got the water from was a mystery.

It was a most desolate period, when the trenches were knee-deep in mud and when casualties mounted by reason of unusual activity on the part of the Huns. But the three friends and their comrades stuck grimly to the work. There were local attacks, and counter-attacks, and night raids, in all of which Ned, Bob and Jerry did their share.

Then, one day, they were given a surprise. Some new recruits were brought up to the front-line trenches, to be initiated, and among them was Noddy Nixon.

"I've come to show you fellows how to get a Hun!" he boasted in his usual style. "Give me a chance, and I'll show you how to fight, though I'd rather be in an aeroplane."

"Truth to tell, I guess he'd rather be back home, but he doesn't dare go," declared Jerry.

Not very much to their delight, the Motor Boys learned that Noddy was to be quartered near them, and he was on duty in the trenches in the post adjoining theirs.

There came a period of fierce attacks on the part of the Huns, when they laid down such an artillery barrage that for three days it was impossible for any relief to come to the men in the trenches, and they had to live on what food they had when the firing began. They did not actually starve, but there was not any too much to eat, and there was a lack of hot things, which were much needed as it rained almost constantly.

By hard work Ned, Bob and Jerry had managed to get together some wood which they kept dry in a niche in the trench, lined with pieces of tin. The wood they used to make a little fire to warm their coffee.

Coming in from several hours of duty one rainy evening, the three chums were anticipating having something hot to drink made over their little fire of cached wood.

But when Bob, who by virtue of his appetite considered himself the cook, went to get the fuel, it was not there.

"Boys, the wood is gone!" he cried.

"Who took it?" demanded Jerry.

Ned inspected the place. He picked up a piece of damp paper, and in the light of his flash torch read the scrawled writing which said:

"Borrowed your wood. Give it back to you some day.

"Noddy Nixon."

For a moment there was silence, and then Jerry burst out with:

"Well, if that isn't just like him—the dirty sneak!"

CHAPTER XIV

A DESPERATE CHANCE

Disappointment rendered the three chums incapable of action for the moment. They just stood and looked at the place where their little store of wood had been hidden. Now it was gone, and with it the hope of a hot supper from that particular source.

"What are we going to do?" asked Bob blankly.

"We ought to go down to the post where that sneak is and get the wood back," declared Ned. "And tell his chums what sort of fellow they have bunking with 'em!"

"No, don't do that," advised Jerry, who had cooled down after his first passionate outburst. "That will make trouble. Noddy would only laugh at us, and some of the others might. It isn't the first time wood has been taken."

"I was just hungry for something hot," sighed Bob, as he thought of the cold rations.

"So was I," added Ned. "Isn't there anything we can do?" he went on.

Jerry looked about. Here and there about the dugout their comrades were eating as best they could, no one, it appeared, having anything hot. It was at a critical period during the fighting, and the commissary and transportation departments were suffering from a temporary breakdown. Still the men had enough to eat, such as it was.

"Well, we might as well have grub now—even if it is cold," said Jerry, after considering matters. "No telling when we'll have to stand off a Hun raid or go into one ourselves, and then we won't have time to eat."

"That's so!" agreed Bob, more cheerfully. "It would be fierce if we didn't have anything to chew on at all. But when I catch that Noddy Nixon—well, he'd better watch his step, that's all."

"He's a coward, and lazy!" declared Ned. "Else he'd rustle his own wood. I had hard work to get that bunch. There was a German sniper who had a pretty fine bead on the place where I saw the sticks, but I went down the trench a way, and began firing at him from there."

"Did you hit him?" asked Bob eagerly.

"No, I didn't expect to. But I drew his attention to that particular spot. He thought a sharpshooter was there, and he laid his plans to get him. That took his attention off the pile of wood, and I sneaked out and got it. Now Noddy Nixon has it!"

"I hope he burns his tongue on the hot soup or coffee or whatever he heats with it," was the most charitable thing Jerry said. And the others echoed this. Their nerves were on edge from the constant fighting and danger they were in, and they were in no mood to be trifled with. And at such times trifles that otherwise would be laughed at assumed large proportions.

However, there was no help for it. The three chums, as did their comrades in the trenches, ate their supper cold, and then, cleaning themselves as best they could from the wet, sticky mud, they prepared to get what sleep they might until it was their turn to go on duty again.

The dugout was as comfortable as any of its kind, but it was not like home, of course, and its accommodations were far short of even the worst camps the Motor Boys had put up at during their many journeys. Still there was not a word of complaint. It was war—war for freedom—and discomforts were laughed at.

"Name of a name, how it rains! as our friends the French say," exclaimed Jerry, as he came into the dugout prepared to turn in, for he had been sent on a message by an officer after supper.

"Hard?" asked Ned, who, like Bob, was in a sort of bunk.

"Hard? I should say so. Look; my tin hat is dented from the drops!" and Jerry took it off and pretended to point out indentations made by the rain drops. He shook his slicker, and a spray of moisture flew about.

"Here! Quit that!" called a tall, lanky soldier from the bunk across from Jerry. "If you want to give a moving picture of a Newfoundland dog go outside! I'm just getting dry."

"Beg your pardon, old man!" exclaimed Jerry. "I didn't realize how wet I was."

He took off some of his garments, hanging them where they might possibly get partly dry by morning, and then turned in. Whether he and his chums would get a peaceful night's sleep or not, depended on the Huns across No Man's Land. If an attack was started it meant that the soldiers in the dugouts, as well as those on guard in the trenches, would have to jump into the fight. With this end in view, every one on turning in for the night had his weapons ready, and few did more than make an apology for undressing. That was left until they went on rest billet. Guns, grenades and gas masks were in readiness for instant use.

But the night passed undisturbed.

"Oh, for some hot coffee!" exclaimed Bob, as he tumbled out the next morning in answer to the call to duty.

69

"Dry up!" ordered Jerry. "You ought to be glad to get it cold!"

"Well, I'll try to be," assented Bob. "Where's Ned?"

"Said he was going to see if he could get a bit of wood for a fire. But if he finds any, which isn't likely, it'll be as wet as a sponge after this rain. Suffering hand grenades! will it ever let up?" cried Jerry, for it was still pouring.

Simple preparations were going on for breakfast. There was no sign yet of any of the carriers with big kettles of hot coffee or soup, and it was evident that the commissary had not yet been reorganized since the last breakdown.

Afterward the boys learned that the reason for the failure of their supplies to arrive was due to the fact that their sector was temporarily cut off by an attempted flanking movement on the part of the Germans. The Americans were in greater danger than they knew, but, at the time, all they thought of was the lack of hot rations.

"Ned ought to come back," remarked Jerry, as he and Bob prepared to eat. "He'll be reported late, and this isn't any time for that. I guess—"

But Jerry did not finish, for just then came a tremendous explosion, so close that for a moment he and Bob thought a Hun shell had been dropped in the dugout near which they were sitting under an improvised shelter.

Instantly the trench was a scene of feverish activity. Everyone expected a raid, and breakfast was hastily set aside, while the soldiers caught up their guns.

"It's all right," an officer called. "Fritz just took a pot shot at one of our trucks out on the road."

"Did he get it, Sir?" asked Jerry.

"I should say so! Look here!"

A curve in the road passed close by this line of trenches. It was a road used to take supplies to another part of the American battleline, and vehicles passed along it only at night, as it was within range of some of the German guns, though fairly well camouflaged. But this auto truck, returning in the early hours of the morning after having delivered a load of ammunition, had been caught by a shell. Afterward it was learned that the truck had broken down on the return trip and that the driver had been delayed in repairing it, so that he had to pass the danger point in daylight.

Whether or not the German battery was on the lookout for just such a chance as this, or whether it was a mere fortuitous opportunity of which advantage was taken, could not be learned. But a shell containing high explosive, though, fortunately for the driver, not a large one, landed near the automobile and shattered it.

This was the detonation which had so startled Jerry and Bob, and now, with others, they looked over the top of the trench at the ruins of the truck. It was blown apart, and the wooden body and wheels were scattered about while the engine was a mere mass of twisted and fused metal.

"Look! They didn't get the driver!" cried Bob, for as he spoke the man in charge of the truck picked himself up from a clump of bushes where he had been tossed, and limped toward the American line. He had escaped death by a miracle.

Then something else attracted the attention of Bob, Jerry, and the others. It was the sight of Ned Slade creeping along toward a pile of splintered wood— all that was left of the demolished truck.

"Who's that? What is he doing?" cried the officer in charge of that part of the trench. "Does he hope to rescue the driver? Can't he see that the man is safe and is coming in? Who is he?"

"Private Slade, Sir," replied Jerry.

"But what is he doing? That's a foolhardy piece of business, trying to reach that truck. It's under the fire of the German trench, as well as within range of their battery. What is he trying to do?"

CHAPTER XV

THE SNIPER

All stood looking from the trench at the actions of Ned Slade.

"Look!" cried Bob, pointing to his chum. "He's picking up pieces of wood!"

"Has he gone crazy?" murmured the officer, peering through his glasses at Private Slade. "Does he think he can salvage anything from the wreck?"

Just what Ned was thinking of was not evident. He moved here and there amid the ruins of the ammunition automobile, picking up bits of wood until his arms could hold no more. It was raining heavily, and when Ned stepped into a puddle the mud and water could be seen to splash.

And then, when Ned could carry no more and turned to come back to his own trench, the Germans, in theirs, suddenly awoke to the chance they had been missing. There were sharp reports, and something besides rain drops splashed into the pools of water all about Ned.

"They're firing at him! He'll be killed!" cried Bob.

"It seems very likely!" said the officer grimly. "Who gave him permission to go out like that, and why did he do it?"

No one answered. No one knew what to say.

And now Ned, aware of his own danger, began to run toward the trench. He came on, stooping over to offer less of a target to the Germans, and he zig-zagged as he leaped forward. But through it all, through the hail of lead, he did not drop the pieces of the demolished truck he had picked up.

The firing from the German lines became hotter, and a machine gun began to splutter.

"It's all up with him now!" said the officer, with something like a groan. "I'll order our guns to shell the Hun trench, but it will be too late!"

He jumped down off the firing step, where he and the others, including Jerry and Bob, were standing, and started for the nearest telephone that connected with a battery.

Just then Ned was seen to stagger.

"He's hit!" some one cried.

But if he was the lad who had taken such a desperate chance did not stop. He dropped a piece of wood, but still he ran on, stooping over, and darting from side to side.

And at last he reached the trench where Bob, Jerry, and his other comrades awaited him. The rain had made the top of the trench slippery, and Ned, striking this while going at full speed, fairly slid down into the ditch, the wood dropping from his arms all about.

"There you are!" he cried, as he recovered himself. "Enough wood for two fires! Now we can have something hot for breakfast! Bob, start the coffee boiling! I'm like you—hungry!"

For a moment the others stood staring at him, and then the officer came back.

"Did they get him?" he cried. "If they did they'll pay for it. We'll wipe out the Hun trench in another minute!"

Then he saw Ned, standing, surrounded by the splintered, wooden parts of the ammunition truck.

"Oh, you're here," said the officer, mechanically, as Ned saluted. "Well, what in the name of General Pershing did you want to do that for?"

"I wanted some wood to make a fire for breakfast, Sir," answered Ned simply. "Some one took our supply last night, and when I saw the truck blown to pieces and noticed that the driver was safe, I thought it a good chance to get some fairly dry fuel. So I took it. Better pick it up though, or it won't be dry long," he added to Jerry, and the latter, with Bob's help, obeyed. Ned had done his share.

The officer stared at Ned as though the young soldier were a new sort of fighter, and then, with a shake of his head, turned away. It was past belief or understanding.

As the three chums moved back to where they had set up an improvised stove, where they could build a fire with the truck pieces Ned had brought in, the ground shook with the thunder of the American guns that soon enforced silence in the German trenches. It was revenge for having fired on Ned.

Technically Ned had been guilty of a breach of the regulations, but though his venture into the open had resulted in a whole battery being sent into action, nothing further was said, officially, of his conduct. Perhaps his bravery was admired by the officer who saw it.

At any rate Ned, Bob and Jerry had a warm breakfast, which they shared with some of their chums, and then the day's duty began. It was performed in the rain, that seemed never-ceasing. The bottom of the trench was a ditch of mud, in spite of the duck boards laid down.

"Too bad Professor Snodgrass isn't here," remarked Ned, as he pulled one foot up from the mud and looked at it with the remark that he wanted to make sure he still had the foot attached to his person.

"Too bad the professor isn't here! Why?" asked Bob.

"Oh, he might find some new kind of bug in this—soup!" and Ned stirred the thick mud in the bottom of the trench with the butt of his gun. "It might be more interesting than seeing how noises affect French crickets."

"Crickets!" cried Jerry. "I feel sorry for any self-respecting cricket that would stay here to be affected. But, speaking of the professor, I wish we could see him again. It would be like hearing from home, and the letters are few and far between."

"That's right," admitted Ned. They had had some missives from their people, and also the girls, Alice, Helen and Mollie, while Bob, in addition, had had a note from Helena Schaeffer, who said she was knitting for the Red Cross. But, of late, no mail had come in.

"I shouldn't be surprised to see the professor walk in on us any day," mused Jerry. "He's likely to do it."

"Then he'd better get a hustle on, or he may not find us here," observed Ned.

"Why not?" Bob inquired.

"Well, there's a rumor that we're soon going to attack again," answered Ned. "And when we go over the top we don't come back to the old trenches. We make new ones. So the professor, if he doesn't come soon, may find we have changed our address."

"Going to make an attack!" Jerry spoke softly. "Well, that's the way to win the war. I hope it will stop raining, though. I hate to fight in the rain."

But still the dreary drizzle kept up, and through it the soldiers plodded in the mud of the trench. It was nearly time for the three chums to be relieved when Ned, who had a post at the right of Jerry, suddenly gave a start, following a distant report.

"What is it?" asked his tall chum.

In answer Ned pointed to a spattery hole in the trench wall behind him.

"The German sniper again," he said. "And I'm going to see if I can't spot him. We've got to get him!"

Ned took off his tin helmet and put it on his bayonet. Then he slowly raised it above the top of the trench, at the spot where the bullet had come in. A moment later there was a vicious "ping!" and the helmet bore a deep indentation.

"Spotted!" cried Ned. "I see where he keeps himself! And now, fellows, if you'll help, we'll get Mr. Fritz Sharpshooter, and get him good! I've got his address now!"

CHAPTER XVI

OVER THE TOP

"We haven't much time," remarked Jerry, as he glanced at the watch on his wrist. "We'll be relieved in five minutes."

"That's long enough," returned Ned, with a grim laugh. "If this fellow who has tried to get me—or one of you—so often, runs true to form, he's done his last shooting. I know where he keeps himself."

"Where?" asked Bob.

Ned took his chums by the arms, and led them a little way down the trench where there was an improvised periscope. It was not being used by the officer in charge just then, and Ned peered through it.

He said nothing for a moment, and then called to Jerry:

"Take a look at that brush pile just inside the first line of German wire."

"I see it," remarked Jerry, after a look through the mirror arrangement.

"Well, that's where Mr. Fritz is keeping himself," said his chum. "It's just in line with the direction from which that last bullet came. I've been thinking for some time that he was hidden there, but I wasn't sure until I saw the flash of his gun as he nearly hit me just now. But now I'll get him!"

"That bush doesn't seem big enough to shelter a man," observed Bob, as he, too, took an observation.

"There's a hole dug under it, and he's hiding in that," said Ned. "At first I thought the sharpshooter was popping at us from some height, and I believe he was, a week or so back. But now he has changed his tactics. He's doing ground sniping, and that bit of bush hasn't any roots."

"What do you mean?" asked Jerry.

"I mean it's a bit of camouflage. The sharpshooter moves it about with him, thinking we'll believe it's natural. He scoops a hole, gets in with only his head sticking out, and puts this bit of foliage in front of him as a screen. Now, Bob, you take your helmet, and when I tell you hold it up on your gun. Jerry, you come with me down the trench a way, and please don't fire until after I do. If I miss, you get him, but I want first shot.

"I want Bob to draw his fire, if he can," explained Ned. "I'll be in reserve to shoot as soon as I see the flash. If I miss you take him. It's got to be nip and tuck, and we'll have to make it a snap shot, for he'll drop back into the hole after he fires."

"Go to it!" advised the tall lad. "I'm with you."

Quickly they made their preparations. While Ned and Jerry went a little way down the trench, Bob took off his helmet and put it on the end of his gun. He then awaited the signal from Ned.

"Show your tin hat!"

Slowly, and simulating as much as possible a soldier raising his head above the top line of the trench, Bob elevated the helmet. Hardly had he done so when there came a sharp crack, and the helmet spun around on the point of the bayonet as a juggler spins a plate on the end of his walking stick.

"Right O!" cried Ned, and, almost in the same detonation as the firing of the German's gun, Ned's rifle spoke. The clump of bushes seemed to spout up into the air, blown by some underground explosion, and then a figure was seen to half leap from what must have been an excavation.

"You got him!" cried Jerry.

"Yes," assented Ned, as he lowered his gun. "You won't have to shoot, old man. Fritz won't do any more pot-hunting."

So that was the end of one German sharpshooter.

The three chums were congratulated by their relief, which came soon after that, on ridding that part of this particular sector of a menace that had long been in evidence. More than one American had been killed or wounded either by this sharpshooter or by one who had adopted the same tactics, and Ned, Bob and Jerry had well earned the thanks of their comrades.

"Have you heard anything more about going over the top soon?" asked Jerry.

"Nothing definite," replied Ned, who had started the rumor. "But don't you feel a sort of tenseness all around—as though something were going to happen?"

"I do," answered Bob. "I think it's going to happen that I'm going to have some chow. I smell it coming!"

"You're a heathen materialist!" declared Ned.

Bob proved a true prophet, for a few minutes later a relief squad came to the dugout with a traveling kitchen, or rather, some of the products of one in the shape of hot beef stew and coffee.

Following the ending of the career of the German sniper, the three Motor Boys, after several strenuous days in the trenches, went back again to a rest billet. There they recuperated, and really enjoyed themselves. There were letters from home to cheer them, and also a communication from Professor Snodgrass.

The little scientist said he had tried in vain to get some trace of the two missing girls, and expressed the hope of seeing the boys soon, to get the benefit of any advice they could give him. He also stated that he was progressing well with his scientific work of noting the effect of terrific noises on insects. But, somehow or other, the Motor Boys did not take as much interest in the pursuit of the scientist as they had formerly.

"The war has changed everything," declared Jerry.

"But, of course, we'll help him find the girls if we can," suggested Ned.

"Oh, of course," agreed his tall chum.

Their stay in the rest camp was made pleasant by the ministrations of the Y. M. C. A. and the Knights of Columbus representatives. The chums and their comrades spent much time in the different huts, where they were entertained and could get hot chocolate, candy or chewing gum—rations not then issued by the army commissary.

"If it wasn't for these organizations war would be a whole lot worse than it is," declared Jerry, as they came from a Y. M. C. A. meeting and moving-picture show one evening.

"And don't forget the Salvation Army!" chimed in Bob. "The fried holes those lassies turn out are the best I ever ate—not excepting those mother used to make."

"Yes, those doughnuts fill a big void, even if they have a hole in the middle," agreed Ned.

But all good things—even Salvation Army doughnuts—come to an end some time, and so did the rest period of the three friends. Back to the trenches they went, to find out that what Ned had predicted was about to happen. An attack of considerable magnitude was in preparation, and it was to be as much of a surprise to the Germans as possible.

"It's going to be over the top all right," declared Jerry, when, one evening, they received their final instructions. The attack, preceded by a brief artillery preparation, was to take place at dawn, the "zero hour" selected.

It was believed, and was proved true as after events showed, that by considerably shortening the artillery fire, the Germans would be unprepared. They were used to the big guns bombarding them for a day or more at a stretch before the infantry came over. This was to be a change.

The night before the attack was a nervous one. Yet those not on duty managed to get some sleep. For many it would be their last.

Then came the general awakening, and the moving of the men along the trenches to the posts assigned to them. Each squad of men was in charge of an officer, commissioned or noncommissioned, and in Jerry's squad were Ned and Bob.

"Go over the top with a rush when you get the signal, which will be three whistles after the barrage has ceased," were the instructions, and Ned, Bob, and Jerry, with their comrades, prepared to do this.

There was a period of tense waiting and then, with a suddenness that shook their nerves and bodies, as well as the whole earth about them, the big guns opened fire.

That the Germans were taken by surprise was evident by the failure to answer. For perhaps five minutes it seemed as though a thousand of the most terrific of thunder storms had been condensed into one.

Then, as suddenly as it had begun, the firing ceased. The "zero hour" had arrived.

Three shrill whistles, repeated from many points, sounded on the now silent but quivering air. Not a German gun had yet awakened.

"Over the top!" came the cry, and the friends, with thousands of other brave lads, scrambled up the ladders from the trenches and started toward the German lines.

CHAPTER XVII

"FRIED HOLES"

Ned, Bob, and Jerry were stationed in a sector which was alternately defending the lines against the Germans and attacking them in that part of the country where the trend of the war eventually led up to the terrific battles of St. Mihiel and the Argonne Forest. But, up to this time, no one had guessed that the whole nature of the war would be so quickly changed with the advent of the Americans, nor was it suspected what terrible fighting would have to be undertaken by our boys; though, of course, they were ready for the worst.

So that the battle in which the Motor Boys and their comrades were now about to engage was merely what was termed a local engagement.

Nevertheless, it meant everything—life and death—to those engaged in it, though there was never a thought of death in the hearts of any of the brave men who went over the top as the big guns ceased thundering and the shrill whistles gave the signal.

"Come on, boys!" yelled Jerry, as he led Bob and Ned forward, followed by the others in the particular squad of which Jerry had charge. "Come on!"

"Yi! Yi! Yip!" screamed a young giant from the South, as he leaped ahead of some of his chums to the side of Jerry. "Show the Fritzies how we fight!"

And together he and Jerry rushed on, followed by Ned and Bob—a quartette acting as one man.

It was the first really big battle in which the Cresville chums had taken part. They had been out on skirmish work and on night patrol, and they had come in conflict with parties of Germans, but no large bodies. They had even each been wounded slightly, but never before, in all their lives, had they had a part in such a hailstorm of death, such a turmoil of blood, mud, smoke, gas and flying bullets as now. On and over the rough shell-pitted ground they rushed toward the German trenches. On they rushed in the gray dawn of the morning, firing as they ran, hardly stopping to take aim, for they could see the gray, indefinite mass before them, and knew they were the German troops who had rushed out of their trenches to meet the onslaught.

At first the attack had been a surprise—a surprise so great that the Germans could not, at the beginning, reply even with adequate rifle fire, to say nothing of artillery and machine guns.

But, in a moment, seemingly, all this was changed. Tongues and slivers of fire began to spit out from the gray ranks opposing the Americans. There was a snarl of the lighter artillery guns, the spiteful bark of the rifles and the wicked rat-a-tat-tat of the machine guns, which the Germans depended on, more than on anything else, to stop a rush of our infantry.

Half way across No Man's Land rushed Ned, Bob, and Jerry, with their cheering, madly yelling comrades, and then the toll of death began. It was the fortune of war. Those that lived by rifles and bayonets must perish by them, and for the deaths that they exacted of the Huns their lives were exacted in return.

Jerry, who with grim-set face and blazing eyes rushed on at the side of the tall Southern giant, heard a dull thud. Then came a sort of gasping, choking cry that was audible even above the horrid din of battle. Jerry, in a glance, saw his big comrade crumple up in a heap, the whole front of his body torn away by a piece of shell. And for one terrible instant Jerry felt that he, himself, must fall there, too, so terrible was the sight. But he nerved himself to go on, and a backward glance showed that Bob had to leap over the dead body of the lad who but a moment before was yelling encouragement to others.

But it was war, and it had to be.

On and on they rushed. Now they were at the first line of the German barbed wire. Some of it had been cut by the swift firing of shrapnel before the troops came from their trenches. But enough remained to be a hindrance, and quickly the men with cutters surged forward to open the way.

It was while the Americans were held up here that the Germans took fearful and heavy toll of them with their machine guns, which were now sputtering with terrific firing. Scores of brave men went down, some never to rise again. Others, only slightly wounded, staggered for a minute, paused behind some dead comrade's body to adjust a bandage, and then went on.

Forward they rushed. Through the barbed wire now, trampling down the cruel strands, never heeding the bleeding wounds it tore in them, never heeding the storm of bullets, minding not the burst of shrapnel or high explosive.

On and on they went, yelling and shouting; maddened with righteous anger against a ruthless foe. Forward once more. Somehow, though how they did it they never knew, Ned, Bob, and Jerry stuck close to one another. Since the death of the Southerner the three chums were in line together, and stormed on. Their rifles were hot in their hands, but still they fired.

"The first-line trenches!" yelled Ned, as he pointed through the smoke.

And there, indeed, they were. They had passed over No Man's Land through a storm of death which held many back. They had mastered the barrier of the wire, and now were at the first line of the German defense. And so fierce and terrible had been the rush of the Americans the Germans had fallen back, so that, save for lifeless gray bodies, the trenches were unoccupied.

"Forward! Forward! Don't stop! Go on!" yelled the officers.

A certain objective had been set, and the commanders were fearful lest the troops, thinking that to capture the first German trenches was enough, would stop there.

But they need not have been apprehensive. The boys of Uncle Sam were not of that sort. They wanted to come in closer contact with the Boches. And they did.

On over the first-line trenches they rushed, but now the fighting became hotter, for they were in the midst of machine-gun nests, placed there for just such a contingency. Death was on every side now—horrible death. A bullet clipped Jerry's ear, but he only laughed—half madly and unconsciously, no doubt—and rushed on. A man was killed in front of him, and, falling forward, tripped the tall lad, so that, for one terrible instant Bob and Ned thought their chum had been killed. But Jerry sprang up again, and, seeing a knot of Germans just ahead of him, tossed a hand grenade among them. As a wisp of fog shuts out a view, so the smoke of the grenade hid the group of Huns for a moment. And when a swirl of the air lifted the smoke curtain, a gray heap on the ground was all that remained. It was like some vision of the night, constantly changing.

On and on they rushed, shouting and shooting, yelling and being yelled at. They panted for breath, their tongues clove to their dry mouths, they suffered horribly for water, but there was only blood about them.

Forward they surged. So great was the first rush that they fairly were carried—it did not seem that they took themselves—beyond the last of that particular line of German trenches. Now they were actually on the open ground beyond—the space where the Huns had their reserves, and these were now quickly thrown into the battle.

Clip after clip of cartridges had been used by the boys, and they were drawing on their reserve supply now. But the battle was not going with the same rush. The Germans were holding even as a desperate eleven holds when it is on its own goal line and the opponents are madly striving to shove it over and out of the way, that a touchdown may be made.

Following the instructions they had received, the Americans began to look for what shelter they could find—a hole in the ground, a heap of dirt, the body of some fallen man, a slain horse, a heap of rubbish, a dismantled machine gun, anything that, for a time, would fend off a bullet.

The first, or shock-wave, of troops had gotten as far as it was advisable to go, and they must wait a moment for reinforcements and for the artillery to come up. So it was that they threw themselves flat, to escape the storm of bullets that drove into their very faces.

There was no question, now, of surprising the enemy. He was fully awake to his danger, and had rushed all his available troops into the conflict. He had an unusually large number of machine guns, and on these he depended more than on artillery or rifle fire to break up the attack. And nothing more effectual could have been chosen. Only, the Americans were determined not to be stopped.

Hastily they began entrenching, digging shallow ditches in which to find shelter. It does not take much of a mound of earth to provide a shield against rifle or machine-gun bullets, and in ten minutes an advancing body of troops can provide themselves with temporary protection, while in half an hour they can almost be in trenches, though these are not as deep as the permanent ones.

While part of the advancing Americans still maintained a fusillade from their rifles and from a few machine guns that had been rushed up, others used the intrenching tools. Then, when all were under temporary shelter, they began assaulting the Boches from their vantage places.

But now the Germans had begun to fight back with their artillery, only, fortunately for Ned, Bob, and Jerry, and their comrades, the range was not yet ascertained, so that the shots flew well over their heads. The shells landed back of the American trenches which had been abandoned when the order came to go over the top, and as this ground was temporarily vacant no great harm was done.

"There go our guns again!" cried Ned into Jerry's ear, as he lay stretched out beside his tall chum.

"Yes. They're trying to drive the Huns back so we can go on. We've got to get farther than this."

The battle was now one of longer range, the first fierceness of the infantry having spent itself. Indeed, the men were practically out of ammunition, though a reserve stock was being rushed to them under the cover of the American guns.

A considerable space, corresponding to No Man's Land, separated the two lines, and over the heads of the prostrate men flew the shells of their respective batteries. So, for the time being, except for stray shooting of rifles and machine guns, the two confronting lines of infantry were comparatively safe.

It was during this lull that Bob, looking back from where he was sheltered by a little hill of earth and stones, uttered a cry.

"What's the matter?" asked Jerry quickly. "Are you hit, Chunky?"

"Hit? No! But look there! Fried holes! See 'em!"

For an instant both Ned and Jerry thought that Bob had been seriously hurt, and was out of his head. But they looked to where he pointed and saw a man in the uniform of the Salvation Army coming across the ground over which the Americans had recently stormed. And the intrepid noncombatant carried on either arm a big basket of a type well known to our American fighters.

"Fried holes!" cried Bob. "Fried holes! Salvation Army doughnuts, fellows! I'm going to get some!"

CHAPTER XVIII

THE SCHOOL JANITOR

Just how it happened that the Salvation Army worker had ventured into that place of death none knew, and none stopped to inquire. Probably the man, in his eagerness to serve, did not realize where he was nor how he got there. Naturally he would have been denied permission to go forward during an engagement—that was no time nor place for a noncombatant. But he probably had not asked. He had made his way through a rain of lead and steel to a zone of comparative safety. And there he stood, as if bewildered, with his baskets of cheer on his arms.

And now a sudden change in the battle made the zone of comparative safety one of danger. For the range of the German guns became shorter. The muzzles were being depressed to seek out those intrepid Americans who had rushed over the first Hun trenches and were waiting to rush onward again. This must not be, thought the Huns, and so they sought them out to kill them.

So it was that as Bob spied the "fried holes" the dispenser of them gave a start as a bullet or a piece of shell flew close to his head. He was in grave danger now, and realized it. But he did not falter. He gave one backward glance, not with an idea of retreating, that is sure, but to see if there were any near him in that direction whom he might serve. Then he saw the prone lines ahead of him.

"Me for some of those!" yelled Bob, as he rose from his improvised trench.

"Lie still, you chump!" shouted Ned. "Do you want to be killed?"

"No more than you did when you got the wood from the busted truck," was the answer. "But I've got to have some of those doughnuts!"

And Bob, never heeding the fact that he would be a shining target for the guns of the Germans, started to run toward the Salvation Army man.

Some of the officers, from where they were stationed among the troops, saw him.

"Come back! Come back! Who is he? What's he doing? Is he going to desert in the face of the enemy?" were some of the commands and cries.

But it needed only a glance to show that Bob never had a notion of deserting. He ran toward the man with the baskets of doughnuts on his arms. Crisp, golden-brown doughnuts they were, fresh from one of the traveling kitchens where, behind the lines, the Salvation Army lassies made

85

them—a devoted service that will never be forgotten, but will rank with that of the Red Cross and be immortal.

And now, as might have been expected, the Germans saw the two figures—the only upright ones in that particular neighborhood. And the inevitable followed. They were fired at.

Both offered good marks, but Fate, Providence, or whatever you choose to call it, favored them, or else the Germans were wretched shots, which last, in a measure, is known to be true.

At any rate, Bob and the Salvation Army man met and Bob took charge of one of the baskets of doughnuts. That, too, was to be expected.

"Come on—run for it!" yelled the stout lad. "This place is getting hot!"

And indeed it was, for all about their feet were little spurts of earth, showing where the bullets were striking. And together they ran on toward the war-worn, weary figures of the men in the shallow trenches. Straight to where he had left his comrades Bob led the brave man, and they were received with a cheer.

Though it was desperately against all orders and discipline for Bob to do what he had done, not an officer rebuked him. And then the "fried holes" were quickly handed out to the fortunate ones in that section of the line, the officers refusing any, so that the weary men might have some little refreshment.

"Halves only—each man only take a half!" cried Ned, when he saw how many men there were and how few—in spite of the two big baskets—the doughnuts were.

Bob looked a trifle crestfallen, but he agreed with a smile, and to his eternal credit be it said that when he broke the one doughnut he saved for himself, and it came apart in two unequal pieces, he gave the larger section to a comrade on his right.

"Bravo, Chunky!" said Jerry softly, as he observed.

And then, as if in horrible contrast to this peaceful scene, the battle began again.

"Forward!" came the orders, and the three chums, with their comrades, sprang from their shelter.

And as Bob left the shallow hole he had dug for himself to see what became of the Salvation Army man, he saw him roll gently over on his side, a little hole in his forehead showing where death had entered from one of the hundreds of bullets that were now sweeping down among the troops. But there was a smile on his lips.

And there died a very brave and gallant gentleman.

Burst and roar and rumble and thunder and shriek and yell and cry and sob succeeded, accompanied and overlapped one another. The battle was on again in all its horrid fury.

Forward rushed the troops, freshened by their rest, with more ammunition of death. Forward they rushed, driving the Germans back, out of the trenches improvised by the Huns. Forward they rushed while the American guns lifted the barrage to protect them, and the German cannon crashed out their answer.

On they went, stumbling, falling, getting up again some of them, never rising again many of them. Bloody and mud-stained, powder-grimed and sweat-marked, torn and panting, cut and bruised, with dry tongues that swelled in their blackened mouths. With eyes that saw nothing and everything—the sight of comrades torn to pieces beside them, the falling of beloved officers, the tearing of great holes in the ranks, and the closing of those holes by a living wall of others who offered themselves for the sacrifice.

Forward they rushed, shouting and firing, tossing hand grenades into the midst of the dust-gray bodies of the Huns that opposed them. Onward they leaped and ran and staggered and jumped, but always onward.

A yell on their left caught the ears of Jerry and his chums.

"Are we giving way?" asked Ned, grimly despairing.

"No! It's the tanks! Look!" screamed Bob.

And the tanks it was. A score of them, great lumbering giants, impervious to everything save heavy guns, on they crawled, smashing concrete machine-gun nests as though they were but collections of vipers' eggs in a field.

These tanks turned the tide of battle at that particular point. For the Germans were putting up a stiff resistance, and were about to launch a counter-attack, as was learned later.

But with the tanks to protect them, to splatter death from their armored machine guns, to spread terror and fear among the Huns, the day was saved.

On rushed the Americans, Ned, Bob, and Jerry among them, while all about them thundered the big guns, rattled the rifles, adding their din to the tat-a-tat-tat of the machine guns.

And then the Germans, unable to withstand this withering fire and being inadequately supported by their artillery, broke in confusion and ran—ran to escape the terrible death that awaited them from the avengers of a world dishonored by the Boches.

Wave after wave of storming troops now surged over the positions lately occupied in force by the Germans. Up the wooded slopes they swept, taking possession of dominant heights so long desired. The objective was more than won, and the American position much improved.

The fury of the fighting began to die away. But it was still terrific in spots, for there were many machine-gun nests left behind when the Huns retreated, and the holders of them were told to die at their posts. Many did.

When Ned, Bob, Jerry, and some of their comrades, led by an officer, approached one of the dugouts there was no sign of life. It had been spouting death from a machine gun but a little while before, however.

"Look out!" some one shouted. "Maybe they're playing possum!"

And so it was, for as the group advanced there was a burst of fire, and half a dozen men went down. Ned and Bob had a vision of Jerry crumpling up at the very entrance of the dugout, and their hearts seemed to stop beating.

"Drive 'em out! Kill the Boches! Wipe 'em up!" yelled the survivors.

With a fierce yell, Ned tossed into the open doorway a hand grenade. It exploded with terrific force, partly wrecking the place, and then in rushed he and his comrades, with gleaming bayonets.

"Kamerad! Kamerad!" came the cowardly appeal from the Germans.

And a moment later out of the dugout where the machine gun had been concealed came four German soldiers, all that was left alive of a company of twenty, and of these four two were badly wounded.

Ned and Bob, seeing that the place, the last of any opposition in that section, was captured, were about to turn back to see if Jerry was still alive, when a second look at one of the German prisoners caused Ned to cry:

"Nick Schmouder!"

"Ja!" came the answer, and then, in German, he asked:

"Who speaks my name?"

"Nick Schmouder!" said Ned again.

"Do you know this man?" asked an officer sharply.

"Yes," answered Ned. "He used to be a janitor at Boxwood Hall, a school I attended."

And the face of Nick Schmouder showed as much wonder as did that of Ned Slade.

CHAPTER XIX

NEWS AT LAST

"Well, well, Nick! To think of meeting you here!" exclaimed Bob.

"Don't speak to the Hun!" some one called, and then, for the first time, Ned and Bob seemed to realize that the little man, with whom they had been on friendly terms at college, was an enemy.

But such was the case. It was only one of many queer incidents of the war, and more than one fighting American found among the prisoners sent back, after he and his comrades had cleaned up a Boche nest, some man he had known back home—a former waiter at a club, perhaps, or a man who delivered his groceries.

"How came you here?" asked Nick Schmouder, with scarcely a trace of German accent, as he and the other prisoners stood with upraised hands, though one of the survivors had to drop his as he fell in a heap because of weakness from his wounds.

"We came here to teach the Kaiser how to walk Spanish," said Bob. "I didn't think you'd fight against us, Nick, after what you learned at Boxwood Hall."

"Ach! I was forced to," was the answer. "I am glad it is over—that I am a prisoner. I did not like this war. I shall be glad when it is over and you have won. It is terrible! Listen, I will a secret tell," and he did not seem afraid of the effect it might have on his apathetic comrades. "Every time I shoot the machine gun I point it at the ground so it will kill no Americans. I do not want to kill them."

"Hum, that's a good story to tell now!" said the incredulous officer. "Take 'em to the rear with the other prisoners. Wait, though, this one can't walk. He'll have to have a stretcher. I'll have his wounds patched up. But take the others back. Corporal Hopkins!" he called.

"Corporal Hopkins is wounded, Sir," reported Ned, with a catch in his voice. "He may be dead. He fell just as we stormed this place, Sir!"

"Oh, I did not know that. See to him at once. Here!" he called to some stretcher-bearers who were coming up, "we may need you!"

They hurried forward, and, leaving Nick Schmouder and the other German prisoners under guard, the officer, with Ned, Bob, and some other Americans, went back to where Jerry had been seen to fall. It was just outside of a little defile leading to the dugout where the machine gun had wrought such havoc.

"There—there he is!" faltered Ned, as he pointed to the crumpled-up body of his chum, and Bob turned his face away, for it seemed to be the end of Jerry Hopkins.

There was blood on Jerry's head, and blood had seeped out from his right leg, near the knee. Poor Jerry lay very still, and about him were heaped others, who were unmistakably dead.

The lieutenant bent over the corporal and made a hasty examination. There was relief on his face—relief which was reflected on the countenances of Ned and Bob as he said:

"He's still alive, but badly hurt, I'm afraid. Take him back as gently as you can."

Ned and Bob helped lift him on to the stretcher. Jerry did not move, and so faint was his breathing that there were times when it seemed to stop altogether.

Desperately as Ned and Bob wanted to go back to the dressing station to learn how it fared with their chum, they must stay on duty in the advanced position they had helped to win. It must be consolidated as much as possible before night, or the Germans might launch a counter offensive.

And so, when the Hun machine gun had been turned about, ready to rake any advancing lines of its recent owners, other measures were taken to insure the holding of the position won at such cost.

"I'd like to have a talk with that Nick," said Bob, as he and Ned paused for a moment in their work of digging trenches.

"Yes, isn't it strange to meet him here like this? If he fired any of the shots that did up Jerry Hopkins, why—"

Ned did not finish, but Bob knew what his chum meant.

Feverishly the Americans worked, and to good purpose, for when darkness began to fall they were in strong front trenches with supporting lines back of them, and the artillery was partly in place. If the Germans wanted to take that particular hill again they would have to work for every inch of it.

And now the commissary department got busy, and hot soup and coffee was rushed up to the well-nigh exhausted men. Never was a meal more welcome.

"But it doesn't taste any better than those doughnuts did," declared Bob, as he sat on a pile of dirt, sipping coffee from a tin cup, his face and hands plastered with mud and other dirt.

"You took an awful chance, though, Chunky," said his chum.

"No more than that Salvation Army man did. He was braver than I, because it was my business to be where I was, and he didn't have to if he didn't want to."

"Well, that's so," agreed Ned. "But say, I'm going to see if we can't find out how Jerry is. If he—if he's—"

But he did not have the heart to finish.

As much had been done as was possible that day, after the terrific battle, and with the arrival of fresh reserves those who had borne the brunt of the fighting were sent to the rear to rest. Ned and Bob were among these, and, obtaining permission, they went to the dressing station to learn Jerry's fate.

Their hearts leaped with joy when they were told that, aside from a bad scalp wound and a bullet through the fleshy part of his leg, their chum was all right.

The high-powered bullets do infinitely less damage than the old-fashioned slower-moving sort, and the wound in Jerry's leg was a clean one.

Not so, however, the cut on his head, which was from a piece of burning shell, making a jagged wound that, however, did not touch the bone.

"He'll be back in line again in three weeks," declared the surgeon to Ned and Bob, and those were the happiest words they ever had heard.

The next morning, after a feverish night in which they slept but little, they were allowed to see Jerry, and they found him in better condition, relatively, than themselves. For he had been given a bath and cleaned after his wounds were dressed, whereas Ned and Bob were still caked with the mud, dirt, and grime of battle. But it was honorable dirt, as a Japanese might say. Most honorable and cherished.

"Well, how about you, old man?" asked Ned, as the Red Cross nurse said they might talk a little to their injured chum.

"Oh, I'm all right. Feel fine! Just knocked out a little. Save a few Huns for me for the next rush."

"Oh, we'll do that all right," agreed Bob. "Too bad you had to get yours just as we won the game."

"We won it, so I hear," observed Jerry.

"Yes, cleaned 'em up," went on Ned. "And whom do you guess we caught in the last batch of prisoners?"

"Not Professor Snodgrass!"

"No. But some one who knows him. Nick Schmouder!" exploded Bob.

"What? Not the janitor at Boxwood Hall? The fellow who helped us get the goat upstairs into the physics class?"

"The same!" laughed Ned; and Jerry chuckled so at the recollection of one of the jokes of their college days that the nurse was forced to say she would order his chums away unless he remained more quiet.

"I'll be good!" promised the tall lad. "But that is rich! How did it happen?"

"Don't know," admitted Ned. "I'm going to have a talk with him if I can."

"Let me know what he says," begged Jerry. "I don't suppose you have heard anything about the professor or his quest for the two girls?"

"No," answered Bob. "I guess he'll never find them. It's worse than looking for a cent down a crack in the boardwalk at Atlantic City. But I don't suppose you could convince the professor of that."

"No," agreed Jerry. "I'm mighty sorry, too. You remember what he said about losing the money he had lent to a friend of his and needing this bequest from Professor Petersen. Well, if you see or hear from him let me know. I won't be able to get about for a week—maybe more."

Bob and Ned stayed until the nurse sent them away, but they promised to call again as soon as allowed. Then, as they were relieved from duty, they went to an officer and received permission to talk to the prisoner, Nick Schmouder, after explaining about him.

The man had been a janitor at Boxwood Hall when Ned, Bob, and Jerry attended there. He had been a good friend to the three chums, and, as mentioned, had assisted them in performing what they were pleased to term a "joke."

The boys had forgotten all about him, and it was with the utmost wonder they met him again under such strange and strenuous circumstances.

"How did you come to get into the war?" asked Bob, as he and Ned talked to the prisoner, who was in a wire cage with hundreds of others.

"Oh, it was an accident, yet. I came back to Germany to see my old father, and I was caught here when the war broke out. I had not served my full time in the army, and so I had to go in again. Ach! how I hate it. But tell me—why are you here?"

"The same reason that brought every other good American over," replied Ned sharply. "We want to wipe Prussian militarism off the face of the earth."

93

"And a good job, I say!" declared Nick Schmouder. "It is like a bad disease germ. One of those bugs Professor Snodgrass used to show me in the microscope. Ah, I wish I was back at Boxwood Hall with him. He was a nice little man."

"Yes, he was," agreed Ned. "And you may see him, if you stay around here."

"See him? Is the professor in the war, too?"

"Not exactly," Bob answered. "He is here on a scientific mission. Something about war noises and insects. But he is after something else, too. A friend of his, Professor Petersen—"

"Professor Emil Petersen?" cried Nick Schmouder in such a strange voice that Ned and Bob stared at him. "Did you say Professor Emil Petersen?"

"I don't know that I mentioned his first name, but it is Emil," answered the stout lad. "Why, do you know him?"

"Know him? Why, he once lived in the same German town where my father and mother lived," declared the former janitor. "They were friends,—my father worked for him and my mother had looked after him when he was sick—and when the professor, who was studying or something, had to go away, he left his two nieces—"

"Two nieces!" burst out Ned and Bob together. "Do you mean Miss Gladys Petersen and Miss Dorothy Gibbs?"

"Yes! Those were the names," announced Schmouder easily. "He left the two nieces with my father and mother. They were nice girls!"

"Listen to that!" cried Ned, thumping Bob on the back. "News at last! We must tell Jerry this!"

CHAPTER XX

A QUEER QUESTION

So unexpected was the news given by the captured Boxwood Hall janitor that for a moment or two Ned and Bob could scarcely believe it. That the information, so much desired and so ardently sought after, should come to them by accident, while, doubtless, Professor Snodgrass was using every energy to that end, seemed scarcely believable. Yet there could be no doubt of it. Still Ned was a bit cautious, and restrained his stout chum from rushing to the hospital to tell Jerry.

"We don't want any mistake in this," remarked Ned. "Are you sure, Nick, that this is the same Professor Petersen whom we mean, the same one Professor Snodgrass means?"

"I don't see how there can be any mistake," declared the former janitor. "I often heard Professor Petersen speak of Professor Snodgrass, and I know him well enough. I could tell him in the dark."

"Yes, I guess that's right," assented Ned.

"But there may be two Professor Petersens—the name is not uncommon in Germany, at any rate."

"There is no mistake," declared Schmouder. "I admit there may be several Professor Petersens, but hardly two who would have nieces named Dorothy Gibbs and Gladys Petersen."

"That seems to clinch it," declared Bob.

"Yes, I guess so," agreed his chum. "But what else can you tell us about them, Nick, and where are the girls now?"

The German prisoner shrugged his shoulders.

"As for where they are now, I do not know," he answered. "My father and mother live in a little town not far from Metz. It was there Professor Petersen came sometimes to study and write his books, when he was not in his own country or in your country, lecturing or visiting Professor Snodgrass.

"Just before this terrible war, which I wish with all my heart I had never seen, Professor Petersen came to this little town, bringing for the first time his two nieces. I happened to be there on a visit—I came to see my parents, and now I wish I hadn't.

"No, I will not say that!" quickly exclaimed the man. "I am glad I saw them; but I wish I had sent for them to come to the United States to see me. It would have been safer for them and me, for we shall lose this war—I can see that."

"You said it!" declared Bob, with energy.

"Tell us all you can," urged Ned. "We have a great interest in finding these girls."

"Well, I am sorry I cannot tell you more," replied Schmouder. "As I said, I came back just before the war broke out, was caught and sent to the army. I saw Professor Petersen in my home town then with the two young ladies. There was some story about his having been reconciled to them after a long estrangement, but I did not pay much attention to that.

"All I know is that I saw the young ladies and knew they were the nieces of the professor. They had been traveling in France and Germany, it was said. Then the professor left just before war was declared. He suspected it was coming, and said he had certain investigations he wished to make before the fighting started. He left the two young ladies in charge of my father and mother, telling them he would be back as soon as he could, and that, thereafter, he would look after them."

"What happened next?" asked Bob.

"The war," answered Schmouder succinctly. "That spoiled everything. I had to go away and leave my parents. What has become of them I do not know."

"Haven't you heard from them?" asked Ned.

"Not lately, no. Soon after I was forced to join the army I had a letter, in which they told me they were going farther into Germany to be safer."

"And what about the two girls and Professor Petersen?" Bob queried.

"What happened to Professor Petersen I cannot tell you," was the answer. "As for his two nieces, my father wrote that they had gone on some scientific expedition shortly after the professor left them, and were not expected back for a month."

"Were they scientists too?" asked Ned.

"I believe so," answered the former janitor. "They loved study, as did their uncle. At any rate they, too, went into the interior of Germany just before the war broke out, and what has happened to them I do not know any more than I know what happened to Professor Petersen."

"We can tell you what happened to him," said Ned. "He died in America, and left a lot of money."

"So!" exclaimed Schmouder. "Well, it will do no one any good these terrible days."

"Maybe it will, and perhaps it won't," replied Bob. "At any rate, he left half his fortune to Professor Snodgrass on condition that our friend find the two nieces and give them the other half of the fortune."

"Ach! Well, I shall be glad if the young ladies get something," said Schmouder.

"Yes, but the trouble is they won't get it if they can't be found," said Ned. "And Professor Snodgrass won't get anything, either. Now if you could only tell us where these two girls are to be found, why—"

"That I could not do—no one could in these days!" declared the prisoner earnestly. "I will help you all I can. I am an American at heart, and I hope you will believe me when I say that every gun I fired sent its bullets only into the ground. I could not shoot at my former friends. Germany is no longer a friend to me!"

"Nor to any one else," declared Bob. "Gee! but it's tough to be so near the solution and then to fail."

"Don't give up yet," advised Ned. "We can tell Professor Snodgrass what we have learned, and maybe he can find a way to get in communication with the young ladies. It's a pity Professor Petersen didn't give them half his fortune when he was alive, and save all this bother."

"Yes, it would have been a good idea!" scoffed his chum. "The girls and Professor Snodgrass would have been better off. But, as a rule, people don't do that sort of thing. I haven't noticed your father—nor mine—giving away half of his possessions. However, the money may be lost entirely now. I don't see how it can be paid over, inherited or whatever the term is anyhow, in these days. Maybe the war has wiped out Professor Petersen's fortune."

"I hardly think that," said the former janitor. "He was not a German, and his wealth was not in that country. He was a very careful man, and if he left any money to any one you may be sure it is waiting for them, wherever they are."

"That's the point!" exclaimed Bob. "The money may be all right, but we can't find those for whom it is intended. And if Professor Snodgrass can't locate the girls, all the fortune goes to a humane society."

"Ach! So?" exclaimed Nicholas Schmouder. "Well, it is better that than Germany should get it. Please tell your friends that I did never fire my gun at them—always into the ground," he said wistfully, as the boys turned away from the prisoners' wire cage.

"We'll do the best we can for you," they said. But there was little they could do to make life any easier for their old friend, who, through no fault of his own, was in a bad predicament.

When next they had a chance to visit Jerry the two chums told him all they had heard, and the wounded lad suggested that they should write to Professor Snodgrass at once, urging him to come on and have a talk with Schmouder. This Ned and Bob did, though there was no certainty that their letter would reach the scientist, or that he would be able to obey the instructions in it. They had his last address, but he was, at best, uncertain in his movements, and now, with the great forward movement of the American armies beginning, it was hard for any one to get to the front.

"But we've found out something, anyhow," declared Ned. "The girls are somewhere in Germany, if they are still alive, and it may be possible for Professor Snodgrass to give them half the money and keep the other half for his own necessities."

"Yes, it may, and it may not. I hope it will, though."

Jerry, thanks to the nature of his wounds and to his healthy constitution, made a remarkably quick recovery, and though he was not ready to go back to the front-line trenches when his chums had to report for duty, it was probable that after their next rest period he would join them.

It was hard for Ned and Bob to say good-bye to their chum. They might never meet again, and they knew it. But it was the fortune of war, and had to be borne.

Fate, however, was kind to them, and Ned and Bob were sent to a quiet sector. After some slight skirmishes, which, however, were hard enough on those engaged, they were again sent to the rear to recuperate. There they found Jerry chafing against being kept out of the fighting.

"Feel all right?" asked Ned.

"Sure! Never better. I want to get at the Huns again."

"Didn't hear from Professor Snodgrass, did you?" inquired Bob.

"No. But I wrote to him again. Schmouder has been sent back to the rear to work with other prisoners, but I have his camp location so the professor can interview him if he thinks it needful. And say, a rather queer thing happened while you were away."

"What?" asked Ned.

"Well, Noddy Nixon came to see me."

"He did!" cried Bob. "Well, the nerve of that shrimp! After he took our wood!"

"What did he want?" asked Ned.

"Oh, nothing in particular, as far as I could make out. Just seemed to want to be friendly. Asked me a lot of questions about how I was treated in the hospital and whether I got enough to eat."

"You did, didn't you?" asked Bob.

"Sure. But I don't quite see what Noddy was aiming at. However, I didn't trouble my head much about it until yesterday."

"Why yesterday?" Bob demanded.

"Well, the surgeon who patched me up came and inquired if Noddy was a particular friend of mine."

"Of course you told him he was!" laughed Ned.

"Like fun I did! No, I said I hadn't any use for him, but I didn't go into particulars. After all, Noddy is fighting on our side."

"You mean he's making a bluff at it!" growled Bob. "But go on. Where does the queer part come in?"

"Here," answered Jerry. "The surgeon told me Noddy took him to one side and asked very particularly whether a wound in the hand or one in the foot hurt the most. That's what he wanted to know."

"He did!" cried Ned. "Well, what's queer about that?"

"Don't you see," resumed Jerry, "it looks as though—"

But Jerry never finished that sentence, for as he was speaking came cries of alarm from outside the hospital and the firing of several guns, while some one shouted:

"An air raid! An air raid! The Huns are coming!"

CHAPTER XXI

A VISITOR

Jerry Hopkins, with his two chums and some of the hospital patients who were able to move about, rushed toward the sound of the shouting and firing. Jerry's leg wound was healed, and save for a slight limp he was all right again.

The boys saw a group of soldiers gathered about a battery of guns erected a short time before to repel air raids. And that this was now a time to use the weapons was evident after a glance aloft.

For, hovering just below the clouds, were three big Hun planes, and that they had come over the lines to bomb the American positions was only too evident.

There was no time to stop and inquire how the hostile aircraft had managed to elude the vigilance of the Allied airmen at the front. It was time to act and act promptly, and at once the anti-aircraft batteries opened, while word was quickly telephoned to the nearest aerodrome, so that American, French, or British fliers might ascend to attack the Germans. It was the shooting at the Hun planes with the guns nearest the hospital that had broken in on Jerry's remarks.

"They won't bomb the hospital, will they?" asked Ned, in wonder.

"They're very likely to," declared Jerry. "Then later on they'll claim they couldn't see the red crosses on the roof, or else they'll say they meant to drop bombs on an ammunition dump or a railroad center and they miscalculated the distance—the beasts!"

If the Huns intended to bomb the hospital now it would not be the first time they had done such a dastardly trick. And that they purposed sending down explosives somewhere in the neighborhood was evident from the tactics of the hostile machines.

They flew about, so high above the group of buildings containing the wounded and convalescents as to make it difficult to hit them, and appeared to be waiting their best chance to drop a bomb where it would do the most damage.

Meanwhile, nurses and orderlies were moving out their charges into the open, so there would be less likelihood of their being caught in the collapsed structures.

For a few minutes the scene was one of wild confusion, and then army discipline was established and matters went on as they should. Ned, Bob, and Jerry helped in taking out the wounded, while the gun crews increased their fire at the hostile planes.

Suddenly there was a terrific explosion just in the rear of the hospital. It shook the ground and brought forth screams of agonized apprehension on the part of men suffering from shell shock. But either the bomb was misdirected or the Huns were more merciful than they had been on other similar occasions, for the bomb, dropped from one of the aircraft, only tore a big hole in an adjacent field.

"Too close for comfort, though," declared Ned.

"Our boys are gettin' after 'em!" exclaimed Bob, as he and his chums hurried back into the endangered building to assist in taking out more of the helpless ones.

This was true in two senses, for the fire of the anti-aircraft batteries was increasing, and now several Allied airmen were mounting aloft in their swift machines to give battle to the attacking Huns.

It was high time, too, for now bombs were dropping on all sides of the hospital, and there was no telling when the entire building might go down in ruins. Whether the German airmen were deliberately trying to hit the place where wounded men were being saved from death, or whether they aimed their infernal machines at objects near it, could not be said with certainty.

Fiercer and more rapid became the firing from the anti-aircraft batteries established near the hospital for this very purpose, and more Allied planes took the air, seeking to drive off the invaders.

By this time most of the wounded had been carried out and put under trees, in the open, wherever it was considered safest for them.

Though from the ruthless manner in which the Huns waged war no place was immune from their bombs—even in the neighborhood of a hospital.

"Look! Look!" suddenly cried Ned. "They got one!"

"That's right!" echoed Jerry. "They've brought one down!"

Tumbling over and over, in a fashion no airman, however reckless, would dare to imitate as a ruse, was one of the German planes. It had been hit either by a shell from a battery, or the bullets from one of the machine guns on an Allied plane had found a mark.

Then, as the invading machine continued to fall, out of control, it burst into flames, and a small dark object was seen to detach itself from the mass and fall to one side.

101

"There goes the pilot!" said Bob grimly. "He's done for."

And so he was, and so was his machine. It was a horrible death, but none the less horrible than he had planned for others—and helpless others, too.

"There they go! They've had enough!" shouted Ned, and as he spoke it was seen that the Hun machines, which had been circling about, as though looking for more targets on the ground below, had turned and were speeding toward their own lines, pursued by the American and other machines, eager to visit on them just vengeance.

And then the hospital patients, some of them wounded airmen themselves, watched the battle of the clouds, out of danger now that the Huns were in retreat.

The machines were so high that little could be seen, but some one had a pair of glasses and reported that one of the German craft was disabled and was coming down out of control.

This information afterward proved to be correct. Then during the battle which followed another German machine was set on fire; so that a total of three were destroyed, and another of the six engaged in the raid sent back damaged, and one of its occupants killed.

Nor did the Allied planes come off scatheless. One was shot down and both occupants killed, while another man was wounded. But the hospital had not been bombed, which was the great thing.

"Do you wonder that I'm aching to get back into the fight against such beasts?" asked Jerry, when the patients had once more been carried back to the wards, and Jerry and his chums had resumed their conversation in a quiet place outside.

"Don't blame you a bit," assented Ned. "But we were talking about Noddy Nixon."

"Yes," resumed the tall lad. "I was saying he asked a mighty queer question of the surgeon and I have my own opinion—"

At that moment a smiling Red Cross nurse appeared and said:

"There's a visitor asking to see you, Mr. Hopkins."

"A visitor for me!" exclaimed Jerry.

"Yes, do you wish to see any one?"

"Man or young lady?" asked Ned, with a mischievous smile at his chum.

"Oh, a dear, little, bald-headed man, who peers at you in such a funny way through his big glasses and—"

"Show him in!" cried Ned, Bob and Jerry in one voice.

CHAPTER XXII

AN UNEXPECTED CAPTURE

The smiling Red Cross nurse had no need to mention the name of the visitor. The boys knew him for Professor Snodgrass after that description, which could fit no one else. And the little scientist it proved to be a moment later.

"Ah, here you are, boys!" he murmured, as though he had just parted from them half an hour before, and under ordinary circumstances, instead of the great war being in the background. "I am glad to see you. I want—"

He made a sudden motion toward the smiling, Red Cross nurse, and instinctively she stepped back, with something of a look of alarm on her face.

"One moment—please!" exclaimed the professor. "There is a most beautiful and rare butterfly on your apron. I just want it for my collection," and, a moment later, he had safe in one of his wire boxes the fluttering Papilio.

"Oh, how beautiful!" murmured the nurse. "What are you going to do with the poor thing?"

"Preserve it so that others may gaze on its beauty," answered the professor with a bow. "It will also aid me in my studies. This particular butterfly is one I have long sought, because of the peculiar markings. It is most lucky that I came here to-day."

"Well, it might have been unlucky if you had happened to be hit by one of the German air bombs," said Jerry. "But we're glad to see you. We have good news for you about those two girls."

"Yes, so I understand from your letters. So that janitor has seen them. Well, now I must follow them up and give them their share of the fortune. I came on as soon as I could after hearing from you boys. I thank you for having my interests at heart. Now where can I see this Nick Schmouder and have a talk with him?"

The camp where the German prisoners were detained was not many miles back of the hospital where Jerry had recovered from his wounds, and, as he would be able to travel the next day, and as Bob and Ned could get furloughs, it was decided that the four should make up a party and seek out the former janitor, so that the professor might hear, at first hand, all there was to be said.

These arrangements having been made, transportation provided and the necessary permissions having been secured, the professor and the three

Motor Boys, several hours later, sat down to have a long chat and exchange experiences. Professor Snodgrass told how he was progressing with his work of studying the effects of battle noises on insects, and the boys related their stories of fighting and battles.

"And we thought old Jerry was gone when we saw him go down outside the dugout where we captured Schmouder," finished Ned, as a climax to his story.

"I thought so myself," admitted the tall lad. "But I'm as well as ever, and next week I'll be fighting again. What are your plans, Professor?"

"I must try to find those two young ladies. The military authorities have been very good to me. They have said I can go anywhere I like to study the insects, provided I do nothing that would betray any army secrets. And I have been very careful."

That is he was careful not to disobey his instructions, but that he was anything but careful of himself the boys learned later. They heard stories of how he went up to the very front lines of the fighting, so he might be nearer the big guns, and he took with him cages of insects, noting the effect of the concussions of the great cannons on their nervous systems.

Professor Snodgrass would have laughed had you called him a brave man, but he dared as much for his beloved science as others did for their country's honor. And, moreover, only the age limit kept the professor out of the army.

The journey to the prison camp where Nick Schmouder was held took place the next day, and was accomplished without incident worthy of note.

But if Professor Snodgrass hoped to obtain any more information from the former janitor than the boys had about the two missing girls, he was disappointed. For Nick Schmouder could only repeat what he had already told. He was glad to see Professor Snodgrass, and it was quite pathetic to hear the man tell his story about having always fired his gun into the ground to avoid hurting any of those he called his friends.

"I didn't believe there were any good Germans in Germany any more," said Jerry, "but I guess Nick is pretty near one."

So they listened to his stories, and Professor Snodgrass made notes about the girls. He said he would try to get into communication with them through the parents of the former janitor, though the latter did not know, himself, whether his father and mother were still alive.

"Is it not terrible—awful—this war?" he cried. "I wish all my countrymen were prisoners, and then they could no longer fight, and we would have peace."

"Well, if it keeps on we'll soon have most of the Kaiser's army in a cage like this," declared Ned. "Don't worry—we're going to make a good clean-up of it."

"I hope you do," said Schmouder, and many of his fellow prisoners agreed with him.

At present all the professor could do was to depend on some message getting to the missing girls. As they were not prisoners of war it was thought that perhaps some missive might reach them, though all ordinary communication between Americans and Germany was held up.

The girls, though of Swedish parentage, were citizens of the United States, as the fathers of both were naturalized; therefore, the diplomatic channels of Sweden were closed to them, as the money had been left in Professor Snodgrass' care. The Red Cross might aid, as a last resort, and if that failed all that could be done was to wait until after the war and then seek them out, if the two nieces were still alive.

So, having dispatched several letters by different routes, Professor Snodgrass prepared to spend some time with the boys.

"I might as well study the effect here of noises on insects, as to go back where I was," he said. "Here I shall be nearer those two young ladies, if I can ever find a chance to reach them. We are heading toward Metz, are we not?"

"Yes, and we'll get there," declared Jerry, for by this time enough of General Pershing's plans had developed to show that his armies had this town for one of its objectives. But there was still a long way to go.

True to his determination, Jerry went back to the front with his chums, and Professor Snodgrass, by virtue of special permission, accompanied them. The chums were welcomed by their comrades, and once more took up the life of the trenches.

It was one afternoon, just before time for them to be relieved, that Ned, Bob, and Jerry had their attention drawn to a stretch of No Man's Land in front of them, by hearing some of their comrades say:

"Look at the bug-hunter! What in the name of Billie Bejinks is he doing out there? He'll be bowled over by a German bullet just as sure as guns!"

The three lads looked, and, to their surprise and horror, saw Professor Snodgrass with something supported on his back and partly in his arms, walking across No Man's Land in the direction of the German trenches as unconcernedly as though peace had been declared.

"Look at him!" yelled Ned.

"We've got to get him back!" cried Jerry.

An officer, who had heard the commotion, came in from the nearest dugout and asked:

"Who gave him permission to go out there? Is he deserting?"

Ned, Bob and Jerry on the Firing Line.   Page

"Indeed he isn't, Sir," answered Ned. "I guess he must be trying some experiment, or looking for bugs."

"Well it's likely to be his last experiment," was the grim comment, "and about all he'll find will be bullets. Ah, I was afraid so. Look, they are going to capture him!"

As he spoke the Americans, crouching in their trench, saw three German soldiers leap out of their ditch and advance toward the professor. But the latter did not seem in the least afraid. He walked on, for a moment not observing his enemies, who were approaching from one side. Then suddenly he noticed them.

But he did not run, nor did he show any sign of fear, and then the most unexpected thing happened. The Germans suddenly dropped their rifles. Up in the air went their hands, and then they turned and marched straight for the American lines, the professor following behind, and fairly driving them on in some mysterious way. He had made a most unexpected capture.

CHAPTER XXIII

GREAT PREPARATIONS

Watching him from the security of their trench, Ned, Bob, and Jerry, their comrades, and the officers on duty, could scarcely believe their eyes as they saw what had happened. Yet there was no delusion about it. Professor Snodgrass, rashly venturing across No Man's Land toward the German trenches, was coming back and with three prisoners. As Bob said afterward, it was like the advertisements of the circus which boasted of three rings and innumerable clowns.

"Three prisoners! Count 'em. Three!" Bob yelled.

"Well, for the love of hot chocolate!" cried Jerry, "what does it mean?"

"Search me!" answered Ned, succinctly. "Looks as if he had 'em hypnotized!"

And so it did, for the Huns, as they came nearer, wore on their faces looks of stupefied astonishment.

Straight for the trench where his young friends were, Professor Snodgrass marched his prisoners. He was in great danger, but he did not seem to mind that, or even be aware of it. Doubtless it was the latter, but, as a matter of fact, he was within range of the big guns, as well as within shot of rifles or machine guns.

Of course, though, had the Germans opened fire on the professor from their trenches, they would have run the chance of killing their own three men, captives though the latter were. And, too, had the Huns fired there would have at once been answering fire from the Americans, for the latter gunners were always on the alert, and once word was passed up and down the line that the little "bug-hunter" was out in No Man's Land, every man who knew or who had heard of him was ready with his rifle—Ned, Bob and Jerry among them—ready to take full toll in revenge had he been fired on.

But the German trenches were silent, and for good reason, as was learned later, so the professor marched on with his prisoners, the latter never once looking behind them, but walking with their hands high in the air.

And the little scientist was as unconcerned as though he was on his return from some insect-hunting trip. His appearance was a bit unusual, though, and Ned commented on it.

"What's that thing on his back?" asked the stout lad.

"Looks like a magnified haversack of new design," replied Ned.

"The professor hasn't enlisted, has he?" some one asked Jerry. "Not but what he'd make a fine soldier," was the added comment.

"No, I can't imagine what he has on," Jerry answered. "We'll soon find out, though."

On came the professor, and when he had his prisoners at the edge of the first American trench he exclaimed, with a twinkle in his eyes:

"Here you are! Make yourselves at home! Will some one please take charge of—er—these—specimens?" asked the little scientist, and again his eyes twinkled as he looked at the lieutenant who was in command just then.

"Great guns, man alive! Did you go out to get them?" asked the officer.

"Well, not exactly," was the reply. "These men tried to interfere with me in my work, and I simply told them to mind their own business and get out of the way. Bringing them over here seemed the easiest way to get rid of them, so I marched them along. Now I will go back and finish—"

"Oh, no! Excuse me for seeming to be brusk and arbitrary," said the lieutenant smiling, "but I can't permit you to go back. For our own sake, as well as yours. You might precipitate a general engagement, and while we're not running away from anything like that, we are not looking for it just now. Please stay here."

"Very well, I will," mildly agreed the professor. "Perhaps I can as well continue my studies here. But what shall I do with my—my specimens?" and he nodded toward the Germans.

The prisoners were still standing with uplifted hands, gazing at the professor as if the issue of life and death depended on him as far as they were concerned.

"Tell them they may put down their hands," begged the professor of the lieutenant. "They're in your charge now, and you had better give them orders. Besides, I don't speak their language very well."

"Then how in the world did you get them to surrender?" asked the officer. "How did you, alone, without a gun or a sword, or even a hand grenade, capture three Germans?"

"Well, I fancy it was due to this," and the professor motioned to the strange contrivance on his back. "I threatened them with total annihilation if they didn't do as I said and march for these trenches, and they did. Whether they understood me or not I don't know. But up went their hands and on they came."

"Yes, they came on all right," said the lieutenant. "We saw that. But still I don't understand."

At this one of the prisoners spoke.

"Haf ve der lieutnant's bermission to lower our hants?" he asked, speaking with a deep, guttural accent.

"Yes," said the officer curtly. "But first we'll search you. Go through them," he ordered one of his men, and when an automatic pistol and several hand grenades had been taken from each of the prisoners, their hands were allowed to come down. They uttered sighs of relief.

"Now, how did it happen?" went on the officer.

"Ve surrender to suberior force, und dot iss no disgrace," said the German soldier who had first spoken. "Ven ve saw der little man ve try to capture him. But he turned on us, und by der—vot you call machine—on his back mit total destruction threatened us. As ve did not vant to die—vell, ve surrendered. Dot's all!"

"Ja!" murmured his two companions.

"Yes, I guess that is all," said the lieutenant, smiling grimly. "Take 'em to the rear, to the temporary prisoner-cage," he ordered one of his men. And then, when the Germans, with a last wondering and fearful look at the professor, had gone, the lieutenant, turning to the scientist, asked with a smile:

"What sort of infernal machine have you there, anyhow? Does it generate a new kind of gas?"

The professor laughed and unslung the apparatus from his back, where it was carried by means of straps, like those on a haversack.

"No, it isn't a gas machine," he said. "It's just a little apparatus for taking moving pictures of insects. It's as harmless as the chocolate sodas my friend Bob likes so well. I got it up to take views of grasshoppers and crickets, and I wanted to get some pictures this morning of those insects showing them as they hopped about normally. Then, later, I intended to set the machine out in the open space, and leave it there when heavy firing was going on. I hoped to get contrasting pictures then, and show the effect, if any, of the sound of big guns on the creatures. But those Germans spoiled my plans."

"And I fancy you spoiled theirs," said the lieutenant with a laugh. "So you threatened them with your moving-picture machine, did you?"

"Yes, I couldn't think of anything else to do when I saw them confronting me. So I yelled that my machine was a new product of the war, and that unless they did exactly as I said I would at once destroy them, even down to

110

their finger nails, by a blast of terrible fire from the machine. Fortunately they understood my very poor German, mixed with English as it was."

"Yes, very fortunately," said the lieutenant. "We saw them drop their guns and raise their hands, and couldn't understand. But your machine, harmless as it is, doubtless impressed them as very dangerous."

When Ned, Bob, and Jerry, as well as the others, looked at the apparatus, they could understand why an ignorant man, accustomed to obey and do no thinking, took the picture machine for some terrible engine of war. The Motor Boys themselves had not seen it before, as the professor carried it in sections in his luggage, and had only fitted it together and used it that day.

It consisted of a black box, with numerous wires, wheels, levers and projecting tubes. These latter contained lenses and shutters, but the Germans must have imagined devastating fire could spout from them. And so they had surrendered.

"But I can't understand why the others in the trenches didn't open fire on you," said the officer.

They learned, later, the reason for this. It was because the Germans had retired from that particular part of the line. Whether for strategic reasons, or otherwise, could not be learned, but the three prisoners admitted that they, alone, had been left in the trench.

Their orders were to remain quiet, and not to attack, but if the Americans came out of their trenches in force the German sentries were to fire their rifles, as many hand grenades and machine-gun rounds as possible, and then retreat, if they could, to the next line of trenches.

But when Professor Snodgrass approached the lines alone, the Germans, instead of firing, thought they would capture him, and so the trio advanced stealthily on the scientist. The result has been seen.

"Well, it was a great piece of work," declared the lieutenant. "Not only the capture, but because we learned that the Germans are falling back. This may change our plans somewhat. I must report to headquarters. And you, Professor Snodgrass, had better come with me."

"But what about my insects?"

"They will have to wait, I'm afraid. Besides, there will be no heavy firing now. Later—well, I'm afraid I can't tell you of that now. It's a secret. But I think you'll soon have a chance to hear all the heavy firing you want."

"I wonder what he meant?" asked Ned, of his chums, as the professor, returning his "infernal" insect moving-picture machine to his quarters went away with the officer.

"Maybe we're going to make a big attack," suggested Bob.

"Perhaps," assented Jerry. "I heard some rumors of it. Well, we'll have to wait and see."

They did not have to wait long, for that day began preparations which, to those who understood, indicated that a great attack was imminent.

Great stores of shell and ammunition were brought up under cover of darkness to the firing line. Big guns were shifted in position and well camouflaged. And there also arrived at the front where the Motor Boys were stationed several batteries of those wonderful French seventy-fives, those guns which did so much to win the war, the secret of which the Germans tried in vain to learn.

It was after several days of hard work, during which they saw little of Professor Snodgrass, that Bob, seeking out his chums one afternoon, said:

"Guess what's up!"

"Can't," Ned replied.

"Go on! Tell us!" cried Jerry.

"We're going to have a lot of doughnuts and chocolate candy!" cried Bob.

"Doughnuts!" shouted Jerry.

"Chocolate!" echoed Ned. "Where is it?"

"Safe," laughed Chunky. "I struck a Salvation Army man with an extra supply and I took all he'd give me. They're hidden in the trench, near where we go on duty, and to-night we'll have a feast!"

"Good for you, Chunky!" cried Jerry. "I always said you were all right!"

"Same here!" added Ned.

And that night, when the three chums were about to go on duty in the dismal trenches, Bob led them to a little place he had hollowed out under a rock, and lined with boards. It was a hiding place known to all three.

"We can stick the stuff in our pockets," he said, "and eat it when we get hungry. Things are so upset, getting ready for a big offensive, I guess, that maybe the rations won't come up on time. But we'll be fixed, anyhow."

He opened the secret place, and then, as he reached his hand in and drew it out empty, a queer look came over his face.

"What's the matter?" asked Jerry.

"It's gone!" faltered Bob.

Consternation showed on the faces of all three. Ned and Jerry made a careful examination of the hiding place after Bob. There was no doubt of it— the treasure was gone! And sweets were really a treasure to the men in the trenches.

"Who took 'em?" faltered Bob.

Jerry looked about, flashed his electric pocket lamp, for the trenches were in the shadow now. Suddenly he picked up a knife, and, as he held it in his hand, he exclaimed:

"Noddy Nixon's! He's been up to his rotten tricks again!"

CHAPTER XXIV

"S. I. W."

There seemed no doubt on the subject, at least in the minds of the three Motor Boys. Bob knew full well that he had left the treat of sweet things in the hole in the wall of his trench. Now the hole was empty, and a knife with Noddy Nixon's name on it was picked up at the very spot. It surely indicated that Noddy had been there, and it needed no very discerning mind, after one was acquainted with the character of Nixon, to say that he was the guilty one.

"What'll we do?" gasped Bob.

"Let's go and accuse him and get the stuff away!" suggested Ned. "Maybe he hasn't eaten it all yet."

"Not much chance but what he has," commented Jerry. "It wouldn't last long with him and his crowd. Still I'm in favor of letting him know we're on to his game. Let's go and have it out with him."

But this was not to be. Just as the three chums were about to go from their part of the trench to that where Noddy Nixon was stationed, the signal sounded for Ned, Bob, and Jerry to take their places on official duty.

"Too late!" exclaimed Bob. "We can't reach him now, and he'll eat it all up."

"The pig!" muttered Ned.

And they had to let the matter rest there. They could not ask to be relieved from trench sentry work to go and get back, possibly, doughnuts and chocolate stolen by Noddy Nixon. It was too trivial a matter from a military standpoint, though to Ned, Bob, and Jerry, forced to be on duty during the long, wet, dreary night, it meant a great deal.

But it was another of the fortunes of war, and it had to be borne.

However, it was not as bad as it might have been, for during the night a relief party came along with hot chocolate, and this was grateful to the lads in the trenches.

"But I'll have it out with Noddy to-day!" declared Bob as he and his chums went off duty in the morning. "I'll turn him upside down; that's what I'll do!"

But again his plans went astray, for orders came from headquarters, shifting many of the regiments, and the three friends found themselves on the move, without a chance to see Noddy.

"But his company moves, too," declared Ned, who had made some inquiries. "He's in the same division we are, and we'll see him when we get settled again."

But they did not see Noddy Nixon again for some time, though they heard of him, and under tragic circumstances.

The guess the boys had made about a great offensive was a correct one. The time had come for the turning point in the war, and the backward movement of the British and French was about to stop. The American forces were increasing, and now General Foch was able to put into practice the strategy he had so long waited for. He could attack, and with great hope of succeeding. The turning point had been reached.

There were rumors and all sorts of stories floating around the camp. Ned, Bob and Jerry had been moved to the north and farther toward the great Hindenburg line which was so soon to be pierced, impregnable though the Germans boasted it.

Professor Snodgrass, too, managed, by means of some influence he possessed, to be allowed to accompany that part of the army to which his young friends were attached. He had not ceased his efforts to locate the two girls, but he realized, as did Jerry and his chums, that it was an almost hopeless proceeding now. However, there was still the study of explosive noises on insects to which the professor could devote himself, and he did.

The boys noted, however, that the strain of his uncertain financial situation was telling on the little man. Cheerful as always, and seemingly oblivious to practical affairs, yet there was at times a strained look about his eyes.

"Yes," he said one day in answer to a question Jerry put, "I have enough for my immediate needs. If I do not get back what I lent to my old friend—and I may even lose more, as I endorsed a note for him to cover a loan from another—and if I cannot use what Professor Petersen left me, I shall have before long to give up my work here, however. And, of course, the trip to the Amazon and the investigations there must be given up."

"I am sorry, Professor. Can't we—" began Jerry.

"Tut, tut!" interrupted Professor Snodgrass, with a kindly smile. "We'll no doubt find the girls—I hope so for their sake as well as my own—and perhaps my friend may be able to adjust his affairs, though I fear—Poor man, poor Albert! It will be a dreadful thing for him to lose all he has and be compelled to start the world over again at his age." And Professor Snodgrass walked away, his personal trouble forgotten in sympathy with his friend, the very man who was the cause of his own anxieties and probable losses.

Vast were the preparations that went on for the advance against the enemy. Never was there such a collection of cannon, large and small. Never was there such a store of powder and shell. The back lines were like a hundred arsenals turned into one. Food, too, there was in great quantities, for it has been well said that an army fights on its stomach, and there must be no lack of nourishment when the troops went forward, as they were destined to do.

All these war-like preparations the three chums noted with every manifestation of delight. They wanted to whip the Hun, and whip him well, and all this argued for success. The soldiers knew they would be well backed-up as they went forward, and forward they were going.

Orders were given that every man must look well to himself personally—to his uniform, his belongings, and his weapons. All gas masks were tested, and those in use for some time, or which showed the least defect, were thrown away and new ones issued. There must be no holding up of the advance once it had begun, because of poison gas. And it could not be doubted but what the Germans would use it lavishly.

Rifles and hand grenades, likewise, were looked to. Everything must be in readiness so there would not be an instant of unnecessary delay. But it was the store of cannon and ammunition back of the firing lines that was most amazing.

The three chums, being sent on duty to the rear one day, had a chance to observe some of the measures being taken there to insure the defeat of the Kaiser's troops. The ground was fairly covered with ammunition boxes and shells—well concealed from hostile airmen, of course, even had they been able to pass that far to the rear. And the guns, large and small, lined up ready for the forward movement, were wheel to wheel for miles and miles in extent. The greatest artillery firing in the history of the world was about to take place.

"If the professor wants to see the effect of a rattle-te-bang on his bugs he'll soon get his chance," said Jerry, and his chums could only agree with him.

"I only wish one thing," remarked Bob, as they prepared to go back to the front, after having accomplished their mission.

"What?" asked Ned.

"I'd like to have it out with Noddy Nixon before the big show. I just want to get one whack at him for taking our wood and those doughnuts and cakes of chocolate. Just one whack!"

But this "whack" Bob was destined never to have.

They again went on duty in the trenches. The day of the great offensive was approaching.

Suddenly a shot rang out in the sector near the three Motor Boys. They started, and Ned exclaimed:

"Can that be the signal for the attack?"

"No, it doesn't begin until to-morrow," said Jerry. "That's one of our own men. Guess his rifle went off by accident."

There was a little excitement, but what had caused it the boys could not learn at the time, as they must stay at their posts. But a little later, when their lieutenant came through the trench, Ned, saluting, asked:

"Did one of our sharpshooters get a Hun, Sir?"

"No," was the answer. "It wasn't that. Private Nixon was shot."

"Noddy Nixon shot!" gasped Bob. "How?"

"S. I. W.," was the terse reply of the officer, as he passed on.

CHAPTER XXV

THE BLACK BOX

The three chums, standing in the wet and muddy trench, looked at one another as this significant remark was made. Bob either did not catch what was said, or did not understand, for he asked his companions:

"What did he say?"

"S. I. W.," repeated Jerry.

"Self-inflicted wound," translated Ned. "So Noddy Nixon did that to himself to get out of the big battle! Well, it's just like the coward! I'm glad he isn't in our company!"

"So am I," added Jerry.

"Self-inflicted wound," repeated Bob.

"Well, he's out of the fighting now," declared Ned, "though he'll have the worst time he ever had in his life. He'd better be dead by a Hun shell."

Silence fell upon the three in the trench while, not far from them, they could hear the commotion caused as Noddy was taken away to a hospital. And there, for some time, he remained safely if not comfortably in bed, while his companions endured the mud and the blood of the trenches, meeting death and wounds, or just escaping them by a hair's breadth to drive back the hordes of the Boches.

But over Noddy's cot, and over that of several men on either side of him was a placard with the significant letters:

S. I. W.

"Self-inflicted wound." One of the most terrible tragedies of the war—more tragic, even, than the death of the gallant boys on the day the armistice was signed, yes, within an hour of it. For those letters indicated a disgrace that seldom, if ever, could be wiped out.

Briefly it meant that a soldier afraid of going into action with his comrades, went to some secluded place and, aiming his gun or pistol at some extremity—a hand or a foot—where a wound was likely to be slight and not very painful, pulled the trigger. Then followed the story that a stray German bullet, coming over the top of the trench as the man exposed himself, had done the deed.

But the nature of the wound, the character of the bullet, and, above all, the appearance of the man himself, told the real story. Sometimes the victims would say their weapon went off by accident as they were cleaning it, and this was perhaps worst of all, for it put the canker of doubt into genuine cases of this sort, and there are bound to be some such in every army.

So Noddy was carried away to the hospital, and "S. I. W." was inscribed over his cot.

As to the causes leading up to the self-inflicted wounds they are many and varied. Sometimes a soldier may become fear-crazed, and irresponsible for his act. Other men are just plain "yellow," clear through, and ought never to have gone into the fighting. They should have confessed cowardice at first, though, of course, that would be hard.

Sometimes, though rarely, these "S. I. W." cases "came back." That is, they were given a chance to redeem themselves and went to the fighting front with a song on their lips and undaunted courage in their eyes. And then, if they died doing their duty they were absolved. But it was a desperate chance.

Every one recognized that there was an element of doubt in these cases, but as for Noddy Nixon, when his significant question to the surgeon as to the relative pain of a hand or foot wound was recalled, he was condemned already. He had shot himself slightly in the left foot. He was dishonorably discharged when he was cured, and sent home, and, therefore, did not trouble the Motor Boys again, nor did Bob get his revenge for the stolen articles.

Ned, Bob, and Jerry did not feel much like talking after they learned what had happened. They had no love for Noddy Nixon, and he had treated them exceedingly badly in the past, as well as tormenting them since they had been associated in the army. But they knew that nothing they could have done or said would have been half as effective punishment as that which he had brought on himself. Henceforth, among decent men, he was an outcast; a pariah.

The long night passed. Sentries were changed, a watch was kept to forestall any attack on the part of the Germans, but none came. Save for the occasional clash of a night patrol, or the false alarm of some one on listening post, there was little action during the hours preceding the great offensive.

Their tour of duty ended, Ned, Bob, and Jerry sought rest in the dugout. There, with but few more comforts than in the trenches, they waited until the time should come again for them to go out and take a "mud bath," as Ned called it.

For it rained often, and the trenches never seemed to dry. Still at this stage of the war there were more comforts for the men on the firing line than when France and England first opposed the advance of the gray hordes.

119

"When does the big show start?" asked Ned, as he and his chums came out of the dugout for a few hours' stay farther behind the lines. "I thought the bombardment was to begin this morning."

"Must be delayed for some reason," said Jerry with a yawn. "Come on, let's go somewhere and sit down. We'll know when it's time for the shindig to start."

"Let's see if we can find the professor," suggested Bob. "We may have hard work to get word to him after the fighting begins."

This seemed a good plan, and it was followed. Professor Snodgrass was billeted temporarily in a farmhouse on the edge of a little French village near which the boys were on duty. Thither they went, and found their friend poring over books and papers.

"Well, how goes it?" asked Jerry, after they had all shaken hands.

"Well, indeed," was the answer. "I have not yet found the young ladies, but I expect to, soon. I have heard that Mr. Schmouder, the father of the janitor, who was looking after them, and who knew something of their plans, moved from his home town, outside of Metz, lately, and started farther back into Germany."

"Then I should think it would be harder than ever for you to trace them," suggested Ned.

"No, I think it will be easier," said the professor, but he did not explain how.

"Getting the results you expected from the insect noise campaign, Professor?" asked Jerry.

"Yes, my boy. It is a complete success. I even have some moving pictures taken with my new machine that helped me capture the Germans. Wait, and I will show you."

He seemed as cheerful as though no cloud of financial trouble hung over his head and as though the World War were being fought to give him opportunity to test the effect of noise on the crickets. He turned to a table in his room, and began delving in a mass of things. To get at something he wanted to exhibit to the boys, he set in the middle of the floor a small, black box.

Just as he did that a soldier, evidently an officer of some kind in the French army, stepped into the room, and in a mixture of French and English asked if Professor Snodgrass was there.

"I am he," answered the scientist.

"Ah, zen you will please come with me," said the soldier. "You are wanted at ze headquarters."

"Wanted at headquarters!" repeated the professor. "What for?"

"Zis will explain," and the officer handed a note to Professor Snodgrass.

As the professor read it a smile came over his face.

"Ah, I understand," he said. "I will come at once. Boys, we will let the insect pictures wait a minute. Perhaps you will be interested in my latest discovery. Come, I am ready to go," and he picked up the black box from the floor and stood in waiting.

The officer looked a little dubiously at the object in the professor's hand, and then at the three boys.

"My orders did not include—zem!" he said, indicating Ned, Bob, and Jerry, "nor—zat!" and he pointed to the box.

"This has to come," replied the professor. "It is part of what I proposed. As for my friends, I will be responsible for them."

"Very well, sair!" and the Frenchman bowed and led the way.

Wonderingly the boys followed Professor Snodgrass, and presently found themselves at field headquarters. A company of French soldiers were standing about, and while waiting for the summons to the presence of the headquarters officer who had sent for him, Professor Snodgrass set down on the ground the black box he had brought.

Then he suddenly saw a curious insect crawling along and became intent on its capture. The boys were watching him and paid no attention to the black box until they heard some one yell:

"Look out, boys! It's an infernal machine in there—a bomb! He's a spy and he's going to blow up the whole place. It's an infernal machine—I can hear the buzzing of the battery inside."

An American soldier, who had approached the box and had leaned over to inspect it, leaped away and began running as he cried out his warning. There was consternation among the officers and men outside the headquarters building, and Professor Snodgrass, pausing in his search for the elusive insect, gazed up in surprise at the commotion.

"What has happened?" he asked.

"Some one says there's a bomb in that black box of yours," explained Jerry.

"If there is, get it out of the way! Douse it in water. Throw it away. Look out!" yelled several.

One or two soldiers started for the black box, and others with ready bayonets for the professor, for there had been a number of spies discovered of late in that sector.

"Don't touch that box!" cried the professor. "Don't open it! Keep away from it!"

And, as he hurried toward it, the soldiers leaped back.

CHAPTER XXVI

A DISAPPEARANCE

"Halt!"

It was the ringing voice of one of the officers speaking, and so sharp was the tone that even Professor Snodgrass paused in his movement toward the black box.

"Don't go any further," went on the officer, who stood dominating the scene. "Some one secure that man, and then we'll dispose of the box. Take good care of him!" and he pointed to the scientist.

Ned Slade, Bob Baker, and Jerry Hopkins looked in astonishment at one another. What could it all mean?

"Zere must be some mistake," said the French officer who had escorted the professor to headquarters.

"Mistake? No!" exclaimed the American officer who had ordered a halt in the proceedings. "But it would be a mistake if we let him get near that black box. I heard all that was said. If that is a bomb the best way to let him carry out his plan would be to set it going, even if he destroyed himself. Some spies are capable of that."

"Spy!" cried Jerry, instinctively, forgetting that he was speaking to a superior officer. "Professor Snodgrass isn't a spy!"

"No, I am sure he is not!"

This was another officer speaking, one well known to the professor, and who knew him. In fact, it was this officer who had summoned the former instructor of Boxwood Hall to headquarters.

"Don't arrest the professor," went on the latter officer. "As for his black box, handle it just as he tells you."

"But, Colonel Lacombe," protested the officer who had interfered in the proceedings. "Surely you—"

"I understand it perfectly, Major Dustan," was the smiling reply. "I'm sure you'll find it all a mistake when I explain, or rather, when Professor Snodgrass explains. That is why I sent for him. Will you come this way, if you please, Professor? And bring the black box—"

At that instant the little scientist, who appeared to have recovered his composure on the appearance of his friend, the colonel, pointed to the black box which, all this while, had remained on the ground in front of the group of headquarters buildings.

"Look out!" shouted Professor Snodgrass. "The box has been opened by mistake. They're coming out! Run, everybody!"

Turning, he caught hold of Bob, who was nearest him, and began pulling him along.

The flight of the professor was contagious. Every one near turned and fled, and Jerry, looking over his shoulder, saw what seemed to be a black cloud of smoke coming from the black box.

The heart of the tall, young soldier seemed to fail him. After all, had a mistake been made? Was it possible that a spy was using the innocent and sometimes absent-minded professor for some base and terrible end? Could there have been a substitution made, and one of the harmless boxes of the scientist exchanged for a deadly bomb which he had, unwittingly, introduced at headquarters, so that, exploding, it might kill a number of valuable officers?

These thoughts flashed through Jerry's mind as he ran along beside Ned. The black cloud from the box was becoming more dense.

"Maybe it's only a smoke bomb," thought Jerry. "Or perhaps the powder, or whatever is in it, has become wet, because of so much rain, and is only burning instead of exploding. I hope so."

Then came a yell from some one. It was followed by several other cries of physical distress.

"Maybe it's a new kind of poison gas the Germans have taken this means to set off," mused Jerry as he leaped along. "But I don't smell anything. Could it be possible that spies have played this trick on the professor?"

Jerry well knew that even with all his absent-mindedness and his blind devotion to science, that Professor Snodgrass would never, willingly, do anything to harm the Allied cause.

And yet—

More yells came from the soldiers that had been gathered around the black box and who fled when Professor Snodgrass gave the alarm. And the yells began to come from some of the officers, too. They were not above giving vent to either pain or surprise.

And then suddenly Jerry felt a sharp pain on the back of his neck. At first he thought it might have come from some missile, discharged noiselessly from the black box. He clapped his hand to the seat of the pain and at once became aware that he had struck and crushed some small insect. It came away in his hand, twisting and curling in its death agony, and the pain in Jerry's neck increased.

"Why!" he cried as he saw the bug. "Why, it's a wasp! A wasp!"

"Of course it is!" said Professor Snodgrass, flapping his arms about his head, and Jerry now saw the reason. A number of vicious wasps were buzzing about them.

"They're wasps, with the worst stings of any I ever saw!" yelled the professor. "That's why I want to get away. I was stung by one of them once, and I'll never forget it. Look out! Here come more of 'em!"

There was a cloud of the wasps flying about Bob, Jerry, and the professor now, and the tall lad noted that the insects were also hovering around other soldiers and officers. There was a black cloud of them near the small case that had caused such a scare.

"Was that what was in the black box?" asked Jerry, as he dodged a wasp that seemed about to alight on his nose.

"Yes. Wasps," asserted the scientist. "The most war-like wasps I have been able to discover in this part of Europe. They are a cross breed of the Vespidæ Polistes, Eumenes, and Odynerus, and for stings are not to be equalled."

"Wasps!" cried Jerry, as he swung and swatted at some still buzzing around him. "What in the world did you expect to do with them, Professor Snodgrass? And why did you have them in the black box?"

"I had them to show to one of the headquarters officers," was the answer. "But I think I had better postpone the explanation until we get rid of our pursuers. Let's go under those bushes. I think we shall be safe then," and the professor unceremoniously dived under a clump of shrubbery, an example followed by Jerry and some of the others.

Ned and Bob, who had managed to accompany the professor and their tall chum, were stung several times before they, also, found shelter beneath the thick leaves, and howls of pain from a number of soldiers indicated that they, too, felt the stings of the insects.

For a while there was as bad a rout of the headquarters staff as if the Germans had overwhelmed it. But finally the insects were dispersed, most of them flying off to the woods, while those that remained were beaten off, so that the officers and men began to drift back again. The professor and the Motor Boys came out of hiding, and then curious looks began to be cast at the scientist and the black box, which was now empty. The displaced cover showed how the wasps had gotten out.

"Is this the new weapon for causing a German retreat that you promised to show me?" asked the colonel of the professor, trying not to smile as he put the question.

"Yes," answered Professor Snodgrass, "it is. I am sorry, but I am afraid there are no specimens left to show you. Some one must have tampered with the fastening of the case, and the insects came out."

"I can offer personal testimony that they came out," said the colonel, trying not to squirm. "They came, they saw, and they conquered. And all I have to say is that I thank you for your interest in the matter, but that we shall have to decline to add your new and very efficient, but uncontrollable, weapon to the Allied armament."

"Does that mean you can't use the wasps?" asked the professor.

"I'm afraid it does," said the colonel. "You see they are too uncertain—like the poison gas the Germans first used. It came back on them. The wasps might do that to us."

"Yes," agreed the little scientist, "they might."

And then, as the last of the insects disappeared, and the headquarters staff came back from various places of refuge, Professor Snodgrass explained.

He had long wanted to do something to help the Allied cause, and thought perhaps it might be along the line of his studies of insects. Then the idea of wasps had come to him. He knew the vicious nature of the insects, and how fearlessly they would attack anything in their way. It was his idea that many thousands of the wasps might be propagated in artificial nests and loosed on the German armies preceding an attack by the Allies. The wasps would certainly cause disorder, if not a rout, he thought, and so he had communicated his idea to his friend, the colonel.

That is, he had communicated the fact that he had the idea, but he had not disclosed the nature of the "new weapon," as he called it in a note. Always willing to test anything new, the colonel had sent for the professor, inviting him to bring a model of the "new weapon" with him. The officer supposed the "weapon" might be a gun, projectile or powder.

"The idea was a good one in theory," said Jerry, as he and his chums went back with the professor, who carried the now empty black box.

"And it worked out all right in practice," declared Ned. "I never saw a quicker retreat."

"The only thing that spoils it, as the colonel said," added Bob, "is the inability of a wasp to distinguish between a friend and a foe. If they could be trained, now—"

"We'll delegate that to you," put in Ned.

"No, thanks! I'm stung badly enough as it is."

And the professor, sadly shaking his head over the failure of his scheme, went back to work further on his plan of making moving pictures of insects hopping about under the stimulus of the noise of big guns.

But for many a day the story of the wasps at headquarters was told up and down the firing line.

It was about a week after this, when preparations for the big attack had almost reached completion, that the three chums, having an hour or so to spare, thought to call on Professor Snodgrass. They went to the little house in the French village where he had been staying, and inquired for him.

"He has disappeared, Messieurs," answered the old woman who looked after the place.

"Disappeared!" echoed the boys blankly.

"Yes, Messieurs. He went out yesterday morning without his hat to chase after a butterfly he saw in the garden, and he did not come back. He has disappeared. I am sorry, for he was a nice man, though a trifle queer at times."

"Well, what do you know about that?" gasped Jerry, while his chums looked at him in wondering amazement.

CHAPTER XXVII

ST. MIHIEL

"What are we going to do?" asked Bob.

"What can we do?" Ned returned.

"Let's go after him and bring him back!" exclaimed the excitable Bob. "Maybe the Germans have him!"

"Then we'll not easily get him," said Jerry. "And, as a matter of fact, we can't even try."

"Why not?" asked Ned.

"Because we can't leave. All furloughs have been stopped these last three days. We may go into action any minute. If the professor is in trouble we can't help him."

"That seems hard," murmured Bob.

"It is," agreed Jerry. "But it's the fortune of war. We're here to fight, and we've got to do that when the time comes. It may be that the professor has only wandered off among our own soldiers, or those of the French or English, after a butterfly or some other bug."

"But without his hat!" exclaimed Bob.

"And gone more than a day!" added Ned.

"Those things wouldn't worry him," said Jerry. "Half the time he forgets his hat, and it is midsummer now. As for being gone more than a day, he's often spent longer than that chasing a single flea. He is used to camping out, and he'll get along somehow. We'll just have to let him go, that's all."

"I suppose so," agreed Ned; "but it's too bad."

It was, but there was nothing they could do. The professor might wander into the enemy's territory and be captured, or he might come safely back to the little French village.

"Though if he doesn't come back what are we to do with his things and about Professor Petersen's nieces?" asked Ned.

"The best we can," advised Jerry.

"After the war, if we're alive, we can look for the girls," suggested Bob.

"Pretty slim chance of finding 'em," murmured Ned.

"It wouldn't do much good, anyway, if we can't find the professor. The money was not left to us to divide," was Jerry's comment.

Jerry had spoken truly when he said that all leave had been stopped, for now were beginning the final great assaults of the American and Allied armies that were, if not actually to overwhelm the Huns, at least to approach so nearly that state that there was a distinction without a difference.

And it was well that Ned, Bob, and Jerry returned to their station when they did, for not ten minutes later the general order to move forward was given up and down the long line.

"Forward!" was the battle cry—the watchword that was to guide them all. "Forward!"

Forward they went, against Germany's best troops. Forward against a relentless and almost impregnable foe. Forward in the name of Humanity, Freedom, and Right. Forward all!

And as Ned, Bob, and Jerry marched with their comrades up to the firing lines there began that great movement of American troops which took part in the reduction of the St. Mihiel salient—the wiping out of the great wedge the Germans had driven into France. And with the wiping out of this there began the final battle—the cleaning of the Argonne Forest which brought an end to the war.

For some time General Pershing and his general staff had looked forward to the reduction of the St. Mihiel salient. With that out of the way it meant the concentration of the American divisions in their own zone.

Late in August the line, beginning at Port sur Seille, east of the Moselle, and extending to the west through St. Mihiel, thence north to a point opposite Verdun, was placed under the supervision of the American commander. Later the American sector was extended across the Meuse to the western edge of the Argonne Forest, and included the Second Colonial French, which held the point of the salient and the Seventeenth French Corps, which occupied the heights above Verdun.

As Ned, Bob, and Jerry marched on with their comrades they saw, or became aware of, the immensity of the preparations needed to make this movement a success. For they had to move against a German position second to none in strength. To quote General Pershing:

"The preparation for a complicated operation against the formidable defenses in front of us included the assembling of divisions and of corps of army artillery, transport, aircraft, tanks, ambulances, the location of

129

hospitals, and the molding together of all of the elements of a great modern army with its own railheads, supplied directly by our own Service of Supply. The concentration for this operation, which was to be a surprise, involved the movement, mostly at night, of approximately , troops, and required for its success the most careful attention to every detail.

"The French were generous in giving us assistance in corps and army artillery, with its personnel, and we were confident from the start of our superiority over the enemy in guns of all calibers. Our heavy guns were able to reach Metz and to interfere seriously with German rail movements. The French Independent Air Force was placed under my command which, together with the British bombing squadrons and our air forces, gave us the largest assembly of aviation that had ever been engaged in one operation on the western front."

It must not be imagined that all this great army went forward in a day or two, or that the battle lasted but a short time. On the other hand, it was a fight, tooth and nail, for almost every foot of the way. The battle line from Les Esparages, around the nose of the St. Mihiel salient to the Moselle River was about forty miles, and was greatly strengthened by artificial defenses. This gives some idea of the task ahead of General Pershing. If you will picture to yourself a distance from your own home, as you sit reading this, to some point distant forty miles, in the woods or mountains, and then figure this forty miles occupied by advancing troops, fighting against a ruthless foe, you will have some idea of the battle of St. Mihiel.

And it was forward into this battle that Ned, Bob, and Jerry and their comrades moved. It would be impossible to tell all that happened—of the surging forward into the face of devastating fire; of the men who fell at the sides of the chums, killed or desperately wounded; of the terrible and awful sights they saw. For days they fought on. Gaining ground here, losing, perhaps, a little there, hiding all night in rain-filled shell-holes, being driven out, but going back to recapture them again. On and on they went.

They were weary to death, but they kept on, and, for a wonder, such is sometimes the fortune of war, neither Ned, Bob, nor Jerry was seriously wounded. They received minor knocks, scratches, and bruises, and once Bob's cheek was grazed by a bullet. But they did not have to drop out of the fighting.

And it was fierce! No other word describes it. They fought, and fought, and fought again, onward, ever onward. For they must not stop. The American army did not know that word.

And then, after nearly two weeks of steady fighting, with only such rest for the exhausted troops as was absolutely necessary, came the final stage.

Ned, Bob, and Jerry, staggering from weariness, took their places in line one gray morning.

Suddenly about them thundered great salvos of firing. It shook the very ground. The chums looked at one another in wonder.

"This must be another big show," shouted Jerry. He had to shout to be heard above the noise.

"It is," said Ned.

And it was. It was the final assault against the last of the German defenses in St. Mihiel.

"Forward!" came the cry, given after four hours of the greatest artillery barrage ever laid down. At five o'clock, on the morning of September th, seven American divisions in the front line advanced. They were assisted by tanks, manned by Americans and French, and there were groups of wire-cutters and other groups armed with bangalore torpedoes. "These," says General Pershing, in his report, "went through the successive bands of barbed wire that protected the enemy's front line and support trenches, in irresistible waves on schedule time, breaking down all defenses of an enemy demoralized by the great volume of our artillery fire, and our sudden approach out of the fog."

And forward, in their own modest and humble way, with this great army of liberation went Ned, Bob, and Jerry. Shooting and being shot at they went forward until the iron strength of the foe was broken, and the cry sounded:

"They're running away! We've got 'em beat!"

And thus it was. German troops were giving way in a rout. Let General Pershing tell it in his own simple way:

"Our st Corps advanced to Thiacourt, while our th Corps curved back to the southwest through Nonsard. The d Colonial French Corps made the slight advance required of it on very difficult ground, and the th Corps took its three ridges and repulsed a counter-attack. A rapid march brought reserve regiments of a division of the th Corps into Vigneulles in the early morning, where it linked up with patrols of our th Corps, closing the salient and forming a new line west of Thiacourt to Vigneulles and beyond Fresnes-en-Woevre. At the cost of only , casualties, mostly light, we had taken , prisoners and guns, a great quantity of material, released the inhabitants of many villages from enemy domination, and established our lines in a position to threaten Metz. This signal success of the American First Army in its first offensive was of prime importance. The Allies found they had a formidable army to aid them, and the enemy learned finally that he had one to reckon with."

And that was the battle of St. Mihiel.

CHAPTER XXVIII

IN ARGONNE FOREST

"Well, I reckon we get a rest now, don't we?" asked Bob of his two chums, as they were ordered to report to a certain point with others of their command.

"A rest?" cried Ned. "Say, Chunky, I'm going to take a leaf out of your book and wish for something to eat."

"I guess we'll get that, but I doubt if we get much rest," put in Jerry Hopkins. "I can smell something cooking, but I don't see 'em getting any beds ready for us."

And Jerry proved a true prophet, for there was refreshment for the battle-worn troops—hot food which they very much needed.

"Have we got to fight some more?" asked Bob, as he ate his rations with every indication of appetite.

"I should say so!" cried Jerry. "Why, we've got to take the Argonne Forest yet, and that's going to be worse than this."

And it was.

Without giving his divisions a rest, which he dared not do, General Pershing, on the day after the capture of St. Mihiel, sent some of them toward the area back of the line between the Meuse River and the western edge of the Forest of Argonne. Though the fighting to gain St. Mihiel had been terrific, with this out of the way the German line was still intact from Switzerland to the east of Rheims. The general attack, all along this line, was with the hope of cutting it, and the part assigned to the American armies was, as the hinge of the Allied offensive, directed toward important railway communications of the German armies through Mezieres and Sedan.

Knowing that the Germans realized what it would mean to them to lose the Argonne Forest, General Pershing and his staff made every preparation for success. To this end as much secrecy as possible marked the advance of the Americans.

Says General Pershing:

"We expected to draw the best German divisions to our front, and to consume them, while the enemy was held under grave apprehension lest our attack should break his line, which it was our firm purpose to do."

Ringing words that will go down in history to the honor of America!

And with this advance, fighting as they went, Ned, Bob, and Jerry, and thousands of their brave comrades, dashed forward into what was to be one of the bloodiest and most desperate engagements of the war. To let General Pershing tell the story in part, by quoting again from his wonderful report:

"On the night of September th our troops quietly took the place of the French who thinly held the line in this sector, which had long been inactive. In the attack which began on the th we drove through the barbed-wire entanglements and the sea of shell craters across No Man's Land, mastering all the first-line defenses. Continuing on the th and th, against machine guns and artillery of an increasing number of enemy reserve divisions, we penetrated to a depth of from three to seven miles and took the village of Montfaucon and its commanding hill and Exermont, Gercourt, Cuisy, Septsarges, Malancourt, Ivoiry, Epinonville, Charpentry, Very, and other villages. East of the Meuse one of our divisions, which was with the d Colonial French Corps, captured Marcheville and Rieville, giving further protection to the flank of our main body. We had taken , prisoners, we had gained our point of forcing the battle into the open, and were prepared for the enemy's reaction, which was bound to come, as he had good roads and ample railroad facilities for bringing up his artillery and reserves.

"In the chill rain of dark nights our engineers had to build new roads across spongy, shell-torn areas, repair broken roads beyond No Man's Land, and build bridges. Our gunners, with no thought of sleep, put their shoulders to wheels and drag-ropes to bring their guns through the mire in support of the infantry, now under the increasing fire of the enemy's artillery. Our attack had taken the enemy by surprise, but, quickly recovering himself, he began to fire counter-attacks in strong force, supported by heavy bombardments, with large quantities of gas. From September th until October th we maintained the offensive against patches of woods defended by snipers and continuous lines of machine guns, and pushed forward our guns and transport, seizing strategical points in preparation for further attacks."

And Ned, Bob, and Jerry had an honorable if humble part in all this. Forward they fought their way, now falling back as some fierce German resistance turned into a counter-attack and again rushing on to capture some little wooded knoll or hold some group of trees after the Hun machine gunners had been killed.

That was the worst of the fighting—against the machine guns. They were almost as thick as leaves in this Argonne Forest and the woods offered excellent protection to the enemy.

But it was fight, if not exactly in the open, more nearly so than battles of the trenches, which the Americans hated. It was like being on their own ground, for, though the forest was in France, the trees and bushes were like those in any dense American woods.

"It's like being with the professor on some bug-hunting trip!" yelled Bob, as he and his chums rushed on, firing as they went.

"Except it isn't so healthy," added Jerry. "Look out!" he shouted, and he pulled Bob down into the underbrush beside him only just in time, for there came a burst of bullets from a machine gun, concealed in a clump of trees, and but for Jerry's timely act when he saw it, Bob might have been killed.

Then, with a yell, a company of Americans, with Ned, Bob, and Jerry aiding them, rushed on the Hun nest and wiped it out, turning the machine gun on the gray troops about them.

So the fighting went on, bitterly and terribly, as it had been going on for over a month, for this was now the beginning of October.

There came a lull in the conflict in the immediate neighborhood of the Motor Boys. They sank down exhausted on the ground under the trees, waiting for further commands, for an officer had ordered a halt.

As the captain of the company to which Ned, Bob, and Jerry had been assigned was approaching to gather his men together, a runner came along a scarcely defined path.

He saluted the captain, and talked to him for a moment. Jerry, who was nearest his commander, saw a queer look on the latter's face. Then, as the runner, with his message disappeared into the depths of the forest, the captain turned to his lieutenant, and our heroes heard him say:

"We're cut off!"

"Cut off?"

"Yes, our battalion and another is surrounded here in the Argonne Forest. There are Germans all around us. We're cut off. A runner has just gone to see if he can get through and summon help."

"Surrounded!" was the thought that came to all who heard. "Surrounded by the Germans! Cut off!"

And then, almost as soon as that thought formed came another.

"We'll hold out until help comes or fight our way through!"

And then began the tragic story of the "Lost Battalions."

CHAPTER XXIX

CAPTURED

Just how or why the two battalions became lost and surrounded in the Argonne Forest probably no one will ever know. It was probably a case of the commands rushing on irresistibly to get as far as possible into the fore of the fight, and in going too far through over-zealousness. Or there may have been misunderstandings, which would not be uncommon in such a great battle.

However it was, two American battalions were cut off from their supporting friends, and surrounded by the Germans who, after having been driven out of the woods at a certain point, stormed back and closed the gap through which the two battalions had gone. Thus they were held at the mercy of the Huns.

But, as has been said, there was only one thought in the minds of all—or rather, two. To fight their way back and establish communication with their comrades if possible, or to stand off the attacking Germans until help came.

And then began a terrible time that lasted from October d to October th—a week of terror, death and anguish. But the brave Americans bore it all with fortitude. They had no thought of surrender even when their food gave out and their ammunition was reduced to the last few rounds.

Once it was certain that the two battalions were surrounded by the Germans in the thick woods, a plan of defense was laid out. The commanding officers held a consultation and outlined what they hoped to do. Sending runners for help was one of these. But this plan did not succeed. Most of the runners were either killed or captured. Some may have gotten through, wounded, but for some time it was impossible for the relieving army to locate their lost comrades. Efforts were made to find them by means of aeroplanes flying over the woods, but the growth of trees and bushes was so dense that no observations could be made.

And, all this while, the Germans were firing steadily at the brave men whom they had surrounded in a ring of steel. Mortars and machine guns poured a storm of shot and bullets on them, but the Americans replied in kind, killing and being killed. For terrible toll was taken by the Huns, who had the advantage.

Ned, Bob, and Jerry did their duty as it came to them, as their companions did. Once Jerry, volunteering as a runner from one position to another, to take the place of a man killed, came to a lonely spot in the forest and as he advanced he heard the shrill whine of a bullet near him.

Instinctively he felt where it came from, and thought he had located the German sniper. Dropping into a pile of leaves, as though shot, Jerry watched from under his cap. He saw a Hun cautiously raise his head from behind a distant stump, and that was the last act on the part of that particular German.

Jerry fired from his pistol, prone as he lay, and the shot went true. Then the tall lad resumed his journey, delivered the message and brought back the answer.

The days and nights of terror passed slowly. There was engagement after engagement. Time after time the Americans tried to break through, but were driven back with terrific loss. But the Germans could not approach close enough to wipe them out. Always when the Huns stormed there was such a withering fire from the American guns that the Kaiser's troops fled back to the fastness of the woods.

Then came the sending, under a flag of truce, of the German commander's invitation to surrender. He asked the American commander to give up, to save useless bloodshed, and said the Americans taken prisoner would be well treated.

The American commander sent back an answer which rang with defiance.

And the fighting went on.

It was awful! The food dwindled away as did the ammunition. But still the surrounded battalions—now less than half their original strength—would not surrender.

"What will be the outcome?" asked Bob wearily, as he and his chums, hidden in a shell hole, held their part of the line.

"We'll win! That's what will be the outcome!" cried Jerry fiercely. "We'll show the Huns how we fight!"

There came a terrific burst of firing, and a hail of bullets swept over their heads.

"They're coming on again!" yelled Ned.

The firing increased, but it did not seem to approach nearer. Instead, it appeared to be going away.

"What can it mean?" asked Jerry.

"There's heavy fighting going on over there," and Ned indicated a point in the forest where it was known the Germans were in strong force.

There was activity among those that were left of the two battalions. Last desperate efforts had been made to send runners through the enemy line to regimental headquarters to summon help, but all had been killed or captured. It seemed the end of everything, when this new and heavy firing was heard.

And then, like a drink of cold water to a fever-dying man, a ringing American cheer came through the woods to the ears of the exhausted ones.

"What is it? What is it?" cried Bob. "What does it mean?"

"It means we're rescued!" shouted Jerry, jumping up and swinging his cap, disregarding possible German snipers. "It means the relief has come through!"

The lost battalions were found, the Germans holding them in the forest were killed or driven away, and the remainder of the men were saved.

So ended one of the most dramatic episodes of the war, the losing and finding of these brave men who would not surrender, but preferred death first.

On came the relieving army, and there was rest and food and sleep for the beleaguered ones—and of it all perhaps they needed sleep most, for they had not dared to rest much during that terrible week.

"But it will be something to tell the folks back home," said Bob, as the three chums sat down together, able to eat and talk without the fear of a German bullet or shell.

"Yes, if we ever get there," admitted Ned.

"And, all this while, we haven't heard a word from the professor," said Jerry. "I'm worried about him."

So were his chums, and if they could have seen their friend at that moment their anxiety would have been justified.

For briefly to chronicle the adventures that befell the little scientist: The morning he had wandered from his temporary French boarding place without his hat, he really had gone in pursuit of a strange and rare butterfly.

Then, as so often happened, he became so engrossed in his scientific work that he forgot all about everything else, and, before he knew it, he was miles away from home—or what passed for home in those days.

It was late afternoon when Professor Snodgrass finally captured the butterfly which had eluded him so long, and put it carefully away in a pocket case.

Then he began to think about getting back. His stomach told him it was long past his dinner hour.

Just how it happened he never knew, and probably it would never happen again, but he managed to wander across No Man's Land at a place secluded, and thinly guarded, and found himself behind the German lines.

Professor Snodgrass was not aware of this. He saw only that he was approaching a small French village down a pleasant valley, so far away from the immediate theater of war that the distant guns made but a dull rumble.

At first the little scientist thought it was his own humble village he was coming to, and it was not until he saw some German soldiers about, and noted the queer looks on the faces of the French inhabitants, that he realized his mistake.

As it happened, the big American attack was in progress, and every available soldier was being rushed to the front, the few remaining in this village being among the number. They were preparing to leave.

So that, in their haste to obey orders and get to their firing line, or perhaps because they were too busy to notice one lone little American scientist, no attention was paid to Professor Snodgrass.

When he saw that he was in an unfamiliar village and began to ask questions, he was met with astonished looks, perhaps as much at his peculiar way of speaking French as anything else. But one Frenchman said:

"How did you, an American, manage to get through?"

"I don't know," answered the professor. "But now I want to get back."

"Impossible, Monsieur. But come, I will hide you, if I can. I have some fellow countrymen of yours at my house, or rather, some fellow countrywomen."

"Americans?"

"Yes, two young ladies. They were left behind by a certain German, by name of Louder or Chowder—name of a name—and I looked after them. They will be glad to see you."

"Oh, dear!" said the professor. "Ladies—American ladies—here in this terrible place! I must do what I can for them. Take me to them, please."

And the Frenchman did so, with all the caution he could use. But it was not needed. Events were transpiring that made the Germans think of beginning a retreat instead of capturing one lone United States college professor.

"Here!" exclaimed the Frenchman, as he ushered his new friend into his humble home. "Here are the ladies. I have brought you a fellow countryman," he added, nodding to his guests.

Two girls, whose pretty faces bore worried looks, arose to confront Professor Snodgrass. He bowed, rather flustered as he always was in the presence of women, and then, as he looked intently at the girls, a strange look came over his face.

"Excuse me," he murmured, as he reached for something in his pocket. He took a card from an envelope and, looking at one of his companions, asked:

"Are you Gladys Petersen?"

"I am!" was the surprised answer. "But how—"

"And are you Dorothy Gibbs?" went on the little scientist, turning to the other.

"That is my name, but—"

"Then I have found you," said the little man quietly. "My name is Snodgrass, and I have a letter to you from your uncle, Professor Emil Petersen. He leaves you half his fortune and me the other half. I have been looking everywhere for you, and now I have found you. But I wish the boys were here."

"What boys?" asked Miss Petersen.

Without answering this question the professor explained his errand, and told of his long search for the girls, to their no small astonishment. They were shocked to hear of their uncle's death, but they had, long since, given up all hope of ever sharing in his wealth, even though he had become reconciled to them after the deaths of their parents.

"But it is all true," said Professor Snodgrass. "He wants you to share in his fortune, or rather, he wanted you to, and I am to carry out his wishes as expressed in his will. By so doing I get a fortune for myself. It is really a great relief. But now tell me—how did you girls get here? The last I heard of you was that you were near Metz."

"We were there," answered Miss Petersen; "but the German family with whom we were staying after uncle went away thought the place in danger of capture and left, taking us with them. Finally, after traveling about, they said we had better shift for ourselves, as it was dangerous for any German to befriend any American, which we are. So we did what we could. We tried to make our way to the Allied lines, but this was as far as we could get. Tell me, Professor, do you think the Americans will come?"

"Oh, of course! Yes!" asserted Professor Snodgrass, who would have said anything, just then, to gain time to think, and not to worry the girls. "Of course they'll be here, but perhaps we had better go to meet them."

"Oh, yes! Let's!" cried Dorothy. "Poor Uncle Emil! If he were only here! He was very kind to us."

"Yes, we loved him," added Gladys softly. "He was so much like you, Professor Snodgrass—you remind me very much of him."

"I am glad I do," was the simple answer. "Emil Petersen was a man to be proud of. He was my friend. And now let us consider what is best to do. I think we had better leave."

And so, though only after much protest on the part of the kind Frenchman, who warned them of their danger, the three set out. A hat was provided for Professor Snodgrass. They were going to try to reach the American lines.

"I fear you will all be captured," said their host. "And, if you are, it will go hard with you. The Germans hate the Americans worse than ever since the recent defeat of the Kaiser's best troops. I fear you will not get through."

And they did not. Just as they seemed on the point of success, having reached a French village at a place opposite the Allied line, they were halted as they were about to cross in a secluded spot, and during a lull in the fighting.

In his innocence the professor made no effort to conceal his purpose, and he and the young ladies were turned back, while a German officer, smiling in contempt, said:

"You will do for hostages if the Americans come too close!"

"Oh, are they that near?" cried Dorothy.

"Too near—the pigs!" muttered the officer.

"Oh, I'm so glad!" cried Gladys. "Maybe they'll save us after all!"

But, in spite of her brave words, she looked worried as she and her cousin were led back. As for Professor Snodgrass, he bowed his head. He had failed. Oh, if only the boys had come!

CHAPTER XXX

RECAPTURED

Once more the desperate fighting was resumed. Ned, Bob, and Jerry, after a brief rest, were again thrown into the conflict after their rescue from the dense Forest of Argonne. That wood had not yet all been won, but it was in the way of being. The Germans were fighting their last desperate battles, and full well they knew it. Only a miracle could save them now, and there was no miracle for them.

Not that they did not fight, for they did. The resistance to the American and Allied advance was stiff and formidable, but it was overcome, and immense losses inflicted on the Huns as they made counter-attack after counter-attack.

It was one day, after some of the most severe fighting of the war that they had ever seen, that the battalion, in which Ned, Bob, and Jerry then were, crossed a little stream, driving the desperately defending Germans beyond it, and entered a small French village. When the echo of the shots had died away, and it was seen that the Huns were in full retreat, the three chums and their comrades, at the head of a victorious force, marched down the main street of the quaint and ancient little town.

Forth from their hiding places came the French population, weary and scarred from four years of enemy occupation. Here and there the tricolor, so long hidden, waved in the wind. The hated and dastardly Germans had departed, never, please God, to come again!

Forward, into the recaptured town, marched Ned, Bob, Jerry, and their comrades in arms. With tears in their eyes the French people watched the Americans come. It was the day so long prayed for.

Near one of the half-ruined houses, which had been their abode—their prison, in fact, since their capture,—stood Professor Snodgrass and the two young ladies.

"Oh, can you believe it, Gladys!" exclaimed Miss Gibbs. "It doesn't seem possible, does it, that we are saved?"

"No, but I am beginning to believe that it is not a dream any more. Those American soldiers are real, aren't they?"

"They are, indeed, young ladies," said the professor. "At last I shall be able to go back to my collection, and finish, I hope, the moving pictures of insects under the influence of big guns. Oh, I shall also hope to take you to safety with me," he added, as he thought of his wards. "If only the boys were here!"

"What boys do you mean?" asked Miss Petersen. "You have so often spoken of 'the boys,' but you have never mentioned who they were."

And this was true, for, just as the professor had been on the point of doing so, he and the girls had been captured by the Germans, and, since then, he had not had the heart to speak of his friends.

"Well, I can tell you now," he said as he and the two nieces of Professor Petersen watched the victorious troops go marching by. "There are three boys—three young men, American soldiers who—"

The professor paused, and looked hard at a certain group of marching Americans. He took off his glasses, wiped them, and put them on again to stare with all his power at three youths who swung along with the sang-froid of veterans.

"Why!" exclaimed Professor Snodgrass. "Why—bless my—bless—why, it's Ned, Bob, and Jerry themselves!" he fairly shouted. "Oh, there they are! There are the boys themselves!" and he rushed forward, tears of joy for the moment dimming the glasses he had so carefully cleaned a moment ago.

"There are the boys. Jerry! Ned! Bob! Here I am! And here are the girls! Hurrah! Hurrah for the U. S. A.! Hurrah for President Wilson! Hurrah for General Pershing! Down with the Germans! The United States and the Allies forever! Hurrah!"

There was a laugh in the ranks of the marching Americans. Most of them did not catch all that the little, excited, bald-headed man said, but they laughed at his enthusiasm and loved him. But Ned, Bob, and Jerry heard.

"It's him!" yelled Bob.

"It's the professor!" cried Ned.

"And the girls are with him!" added Jerry.

The lieutenant of the boys' company, seeing that something unusual was in the wind said:

"You may fall out. Join us later. We'll probably stay here a while. This is our objective, and we've made it."

And then the boys fell out and such a reunion as there was!

The stories were told and retold, and Ned, Bob, and Jerry, after having been presented to the young ladies, listened to their accounts of what had happened to them since they were caught in war-torn Europe.

"And do you think we are safe now?" asked Miss Petersen.

"As safe as in a church," declared Bob. "We've come to stay!"

And so the Americans had. As General Pershing, in his report of the operations culminating in the last phase of the Meuse-Argonne battles, said:

"The strategical goal which was our highest hope was gained. We had cut the enemy's main line of communications, and nothing but surrender or an armistice could save his army from complete disaster."

And the armistice of November , , came, bringing an end to the war.

And it also brings to an end this story. Not that the fighting was all over, for there was some after the boys and the professor and his charges were so happily reunited. But the Motor Boys had no further part in it. They remained in the village where they had met the little scientist, as a guard, until the Germans were so far away as to render them harmless.

"And to think you found the girls all by yourself!" exclaimed Ned, as they were talking over the events after the first day of the capture of the French town.

"Well, yes, I did manage to," said the professor, "though I never expected, when I started out for a butterfly that morning, that I'd end up with meeting the girls I so much wanted to see."

"But we were glad to see you," said Miss Gibbs.

"Very," echoed Gladys.

Ned, Bob, and Jerry were very curious to know what branch of scientific study Miss Petersen and Miss Gibbs were interested in, for they remembered that Nick Schmouder had said that they had left his father's home to go further into Germany for some sort of scientific work. It developed, however, that Schmouder, ashamed to confess that, in his fright, he had abandoned the two girls, had made up the story to clear himself of the charge of cowardice and neglect.

"Well, I guess it's all over but the shouting," said Bob, at last. "And now I guess nobody will say anything if I eat."

"We're all with you, Chunky!" cried Ned. "I'm as hungry as—as Bob Baker!"

But of the "shouting," a little must be told. For when the fighting was over, and it was certain that Germany could never resume, when the armistice had been signed and the victorious movement of the Allies into Germany began, Jerry and his chums were called one day before their assembled comrades, and there, much to their surprise, they were each given honorable mention for their acts while on duty with the lost battalions in Argonne Forest. Jerry, for his work as a runner received the Distinguished

Service Cross, and Bob and Ned honorable mention for their part in the desperate fight.

Ned, Bob and Jerry on the Firing Line.   Page

"They ought to decorate Professor Snodgrass for going alone into the enemy's territory and rescuing two young ladies," said Ned, when the cheering was over.

"All I want to do is to get back to my bugs," sighed the little scientist, and he soon had his wish. It might be added that his moving pictures of insects, showing their actions when heavy guns were being fired near them, were very successful, and created a sensation in scientific circles, even though the professor's "wasp-gun" was not adopted.

As soon as it was possible the two young ladies were sent back to the United States with their share of their uncle's wealth, while Professor Snodgrass made plans to use his share in making a full and complete study of the insects of the Amazon. Also, the boys learned later, Professor Snodgrass used a part of his fortune to further assist his old friend, and thus saved the fortunes of this man and enabled him to pay all his debts, including the

"Sure thing!" assented Ned.

What was in store for the boys will be related in the next volume of this "Motor Boys—Second Series." In that we will see how Ned, Bob and Jerry covered themselves with glory by solving a most unusual mystery.

A month or so later the three chums, with other soldiers of the victorious armies, some of them sorely wounded, were sent to a port in France, there to take ship for home.

"And believe me!" exclaimed Bob, with feeling, as he went on board, "France and Europe may be all right, and so are those Salvation Army doughnuts, but give me a piece of mother's cherry pie!"

"So say we all of us!" chanted Ned and Jerry.

And then, as they stood together on deck, the transport began her homeward trip.

THE END

Milton Keynes UK
Ingram Content Group UK Ltd.
UKHW011308210923
429112UK00004B/228